Sally Rides Single

BRIDGET DOONE

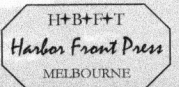
H✦B✦F✦T
Harbor Front Press
MELBOURNE

Sally Rides Single

Copyright © 2020 by Bridget Doone

Harbor Front Press

PO Box 1613

Melbourne, Florida 32901

The characters and events portrayed in this book are fictitious. Any similarity to real persons, living or dead, is coincidental.

ISBN: 978-0-692-15644-5

Published in the United States of America

Cover and layout design Copyright © 2020 by Grzegorz Japoł

(book-cover.design)

For my husband,
who was compelled
to perform the steamy scenes
contained herein . . .
for research purposes of course.

Contents

CHAPTER ONE

Lance Pants Down

"You've never done anal?"

Bill's eyes opened wide with surprise as he choked on his beer.

Perfect.

"So . . . neither as a pitcher . . . or a catcher?" I asked, teasing.

He stiffened. "I'll never be a catcher, THAT's for sure!"

"Sssshhhh," I whispered, raising my chin and pointing it over his shoulder. Two of the big bosses had cozied up to the bar beside him and were having a laugh. I was pretty sure it was about something unrelated to our inappropriate tête-à-tête, but they were within earshot. And while I liked nothing more than messing with Captain Conventional, it's a dangerous game when played in a bar filled almost to capacity with professional colleagues.

Ignoring my concern, Bill leaned in, sliding his arm across the bar towards me until his pinky finger rested against mine. I felt the atoms under my skin along that tiny area of shared contact line up and vibrate in response to his magnetic touch. I backed away from his force field and he countered by perching his right foot on my barstool's footrest. When he angled his knee against mine, his pant leg tickled my calf. He was just about three beers too intimate.

Yeah, I know. I started it.

"I think you're a bit of a tease, and you like to hear yourself talk," he said quietly.

"It's all about the story, Bill. Might as well make it worth telling," I said, standing up and out of his orbit.

I felt a cool hand on my bare shoulder and glanced down at the red and gold Asian-inspired nail design. It was Jody, the administrative assistant for our Operations team.

"I hate to bother you with work right now, but it's Jeff in Montreal on the line. Can you give him five minutes?"

"Sure," I said, happy to leave Bill hanging and focus on something and someone far more important. I hadn't been able to get much traction working at Southeast Atlantic's corporate headquarters in Sydney, Florida. That ladder was congested with too much good ol' boy competition. I'd have to take an unconventional path to promotion and I was convinced impressing Jeff, the head of the Canadian Operations Division, was the ticket.

"Be right back, Bill," I said over my shoulder as I headed away from the bar, concentrating on the call, doing my best to sound confident and competent.

Jeff was concerned the timetable for Phase One of the QuebecNet build-out had slipped. I briefed him on my plan to make up for that lost time, and if it worked, the same strategy could be implemented in the following two phases, bringing the project to completion one month early.

"All right," he said, sounding a little relieved, "I'll set up a conference call so you can give us the details."

"Sounds good. I'll talk to you then." I had other things ready to roll off the tip of my tongue, but I'd learned to fight the urge to keep talking. The engineers I worked with were turned off by what they considered unnecessary chatter. They liked yes or no answers and really just wanted reassurance I knew what I was doing.

Why did it take me so long to figure this out?

I smiled at Jody as I passed the company cell phone to her on my way to the elevator. Alone in my room, I stepped out of my high heels and noticed the spray tan had almost completely faded from my legs. HMMPH! Obviously, I've been working too much, I mused, as I reached into the small hotel refrigerator for a bottle of wine, otherwise I'd have a real tan. I lived right on the Atlantic but I couldn't remember the last time my toes had touched the sand.

I smiled with anticipation as I felt the bottle cap twist loose. This particular Sauvignon Blanc was of the Marlborough, New Zealand variety—predictable, sure, but that's just how I like things. Too bad it's never on happy hour. You always have to pay eight or nine bucks for a glass, even here in Florida where booze is cheap. I remember when Chardonnay was all the rage, and Kathie Lee Gifford named her dog Chardonnay. That's about when I stopped drinking it.

As I pressed my lips to the glass and drew in the liquid mix of citrus, tropical fruit, and crushed herbs, my thoughts turned to Bill. I'd abandoned the poor, starry-eyed fellow at the bar with a promise of my return. Oh well, no matter, he had plenty of company. By now the place would be packed with our fellow engineers. It was the last night of our yearly offsite meeting week, and we were living it up at company expense at the Grand Tropics Orlando.

Reflecting on Bill's priceless reaction to my anal inquest, I giggled. He was such an easy mark. But in hindsight, I never should have started it up with him.

We worked out at the same gym very early almost every morning. He would wave and say hi when he passed by, but he did that with everyone. I wasn't special. I guessed he was younger than me but maybe still in his fifties, just shy of 6 feet tall, broad muscular chest, shaved head, and a golden tan that emphasized his big white smile and Caribbean blue eyes. He had a confident and friendly manner I found extremely appealing.

Monday through Friday, I would study him from the treadmill as he raised and lowered a heavily loaded barbell from his reclined position on a bench. That was his favorite exercise, and he spent lots of time there. Then he'd move to the leg press, which was considerably closer to the treadmill, and I'd count while his quadriceps contracted through three sets of ten. Watching and interacting with him became my prime motivator for going to the gym, and my workouts were decidedly less productive when he wasn't there.

The fantasy always began the same: reaching for his muscular arms, pulling him down on top of me, feeling his bulk and his weight, welcoming his whispers as he maneuvered his legs between mine, nipping at my neck while he fumbled with his zipper.

It was a ridiculous notion, of course. Men in their fifties were looking to harpoon women in their thirties. I knew that firsthand.

Then one day, I took a new water bottle SouthEast Atlantic had given its employees for Earth Day to the gym. It had the company logo on it and something about how SEA was doing its part to save the planet. I wondered if anyone ever fell for that crap. I was doing stomach crunches when he approached. I stopped, lay flat, and looked up at him.

"I have one of those," he said, smiling and pointing at my water bottle. "Do you work for SEA?"

"I do," I said, surprised.

He said he was an engineer at the Riverview location, but that's all I heard. Painfully aware my squatty body was no match for the Chiquita bananas he chatted up between sets, I sucked in my stomach and moved the hair around my head while I watched his mouth move. Then unexpectedly and somewhat awkwardly, he asked me out to lunch that Friday, and despite the possible work complication, I said yes.

His name was Bill Pruitt.

We met at Clams seafood restaurant near the Sydney Square mall. I wore a yellow sundress and high heel sandals, boosting my height to a whopping 5' 3". I had resisted the urge to over-improve on my appearance as he was used to seeing it natural, keeping the makeup light and my curly blonde hair undone. It was just lunch after all, and I didn't want to give off desperate vibes. Nonetheless, when he saw me he uttered that overused phrase:

"Hey, you clean up nice."

I smiled and took the time to look him up and down.

"You too," I responded, but the fact was he didn't look much different, just had on nicer clothes. That's the way it is with guys; no makeup, no hair color, no Botox, no dieting, no nothin'. As long as they have cash in the bank, aging isn't a factor when attempting to plant the parsnip.

I ordered Clams' signature dish, the clam chowder, which I knew was excellent, and a glass of house wine, which I hoped was a decent Sauvignon Blanc. I expected Bill to order a mountain of red meat to feed all that muscle, but he chose a big salad instead.

At 52, Bill was indeed a little younger than me. He had siblings: one single, one married, and one divorced, and spent lots of time with his mother, who lived in exclusive Sundown Beach. Unfortunately, after imparting that benign information, my handsome and charming date heavied the mood with a real deal breaker. His wife had died a couple years back and he was looking for someone to take her place. So, within the first 15 minutes of our first date, I knew it would be our last.

When Bill inquired as to my state of affairs, I jumped at the chance to clarify my intentions while entertaining him with an amusing narrative I had crafted from my own truly heartbreaking experience. It was the first in a compilation of short stories I was working on entitled: *I Shit You Not: Reflections on Life, Love, and Sex After 50, by a Woman Scorned.*

And so began Lance Pants Down.

"Well, after over 30 years of marriage, during which we raised two daughters, my husband, Lance, decided to trade me in for a younger model."

I smirked and shrugged like it was no big deal and spooned a thick hot mound of chowder into my mouth, then chased it with a gulp of the disappointing wine.

Bill had his mouth open, about to shove a forkful of frisée into it, but stopped and looked at me with a confused expression, as if he couldn't understand why a man would do such a thing.

"I shouldn't have been surprised. I mean, I had to beg him for sex, and it didn't seem like he was really into it," I said, looking for a reaction. Unexpectedly, Bill blushed.

That gave me great pleasure.

I took another long draw of the watery wine, anxious to finish it and order something superior. Bill looked down at his veggie delight and the crunching resumed.

"I knew there was nothing physically wrong with him, which was confirmed when I caught him and what's-her-name in our bed doing the forbidden polka."

I chuckled, but Bill didn't think it was funny. He put his fork down and placed his hand over mine.

"I'm sorry," he said, his sincerity barely masking what I knew was real vulnerability. He was the perfect audience and I couldn't help take advantage of it. I kicked it up a notch.

"They were oblivious to the fact they had been caught in flagrante delicto, so I decided to sit in the living room and listen to them go at it. She was faking it pretty good, doing a high pitched, 'Oh yes, Lance, yes.' And then an even more annoying higher pitched, 'Oh Lance, I'm coming, OHHHH, GOD, YESSSSSSS!'"

I stopped my narrative and looked around, suddenly aware I was performing as if on stage, and there were others in the audience besides Bill. I caught the twin stares of an older woman and her friend smiling at me from two tables away. They probably thought I was reenacting that famous scene from *When Harry Met Sally*. Which is funny, since my name is Sally.

Bill resumed noisily masticating his salad, but I had his full attention. Ranch dressing flicked off his fork as he made a rolling, go-forward motion with his hand, urging me on. I brought my voice down and leaned in closer.

"Lance was breathing hard as he did his best to satisfy her, and I listened, surprisingly detached, wondering how I'd feel if right then he had a heart attack. BAMMM!!!!!!"

I slammed my fist on the table, rattling the dishes, and Bill jerked in his seat like he'd been shot.

"Sorry," I said, waving sheepishly at the startled lunching ladies before turning my attention back to my date.

"And then I heard Lance finish."

I sat back and shrugged.

"Meh . . . didn't sound that great. For sure no better than with me."

Bill exhaled and looked like he was about to say something, but I wasn't finished.

"So, about two minutes after the panting stopped, I heard Lance say he was going to get a rum and coke. He asked what's-her-name what she would like and she said, 'Do you have any Chardonnay?'"

I mimicked her request with a whiny, immature voice and rolled my eyes. Bill smiled and nodded. Then, as if he remembered this was supposed to be a sad story, he frowned and shook his head.

"So Lance walks out of the bedroom in his boxers, laughing, and says, 'I guarantee we don't have Chardonnay. How about Sauvignon Blanc?' And then he sees me sitting on the couch. He freezes with that cliché, deer-in-the-headlights look. I told him to grab a suitcase and start packing."

As if he sensed this was the end of the narrative, Bill readied to ask me a question but hesitated, giving me the opportunity to finish my story uninterrupted.

"And then what's-her-name came into the room wearing Lance's blue oxford button-down shirt. Her long blonde hair was pink-tipped back then, and I thought, Holy crap, just how young is she?"

I swallowed hard, the pain and embarrassment I'd left out of my recitation attempting to rear its ugly head. I focused and regained my momentum.

"You'd think she'd feel just awful and apologize, but no, she looked quite pleased with herself, like she knew she'd won. She walked back into the bedroom to get her things and told Lance she'd wait for him outside."

Anxious to get a word in, Bill put his hand up and took a sip of water to help force the mouthful of garden down his gullet. I rushed in before he could kill the rhythm between the climax and the denouement.

"That was about a year ago, Bill. At this point in my life, all I want from a man is sex and a lot of it. I'll never be monogamous again."

I looked down, suppressing a self-congratulatory smile, and started eating my chowder, which was cold. But it didn't matter. I nailed the story.

Bill was staring across his salad at me. There was a long pause as he waited to make sure there wouldn't be another preemptive strike.

"Wow," he finally said. "I don't know which is more surprising: the story itself or the way you told it."

It felt like applause.

But things got pretty quiet after that, and shortly thereafter, he picked up the check and we left. We walked to my car in silence, then unexpectedly, he reached for my hand.

"Thanks, Sally, it was really . . . well . . . interesting."

Before I could say likewise I'm sure, Bill pulled me closer and kissed me on the cheek. I felt a sort of buzzing when his lips made contact and then a kind of electric shock. Reflexively, I reached up with both hands and squeezed his big biceps, just like I'd dreamed of doing so many times before. In response, his right hand shot to the back of my upper left leg, lifting it, coaxing my heel around his calf as he gently pressed me backwards against the car. His cheek was touching mine, and I could feel his breath on my ear and the outline of his Little Admiral through my sundress.

I'm sure this odd embrace lasted only seconds, but it felt much longer. It felt . . . wonderful. He stepped back, and we smiled a knowing smile at each other, an unspoken bidirectional acknowledgement that under different circumstances, this could be something.

CHAPTER TWO

We've Got Your Back

On the Monday after our ill-fated lunch, I skipped the gym and, once at work, spoke with my Engineering Manager about my hours. Soon after, they were officially changed. I would start work later in the day, which meant I didn't have to get up so early in the morning. Which meant I wouldn't be at the gym so early in the morning. Which meant I wouldn't see Bill. As charming and attractive as he was, our disparate goals made any further effort futile.

The week went by with no calls, emails, or texts from him. Obviously, he knew I wasn't the one, so why waste time. I was surprised he wasn't already married. Didn't he know about all those find-me-a-wife-dot-com websites? Then on Friday, an instant message appeared.

Bill: missed u at the gym this week. u ok?

Me: yeah I changed my hours. i go in later now

Bill: u didn't change them cuz of me right?

Me: no i don't like getting up so early

Bill: have time for a call?

Me: no just going to a meeting - ping u later

Bill: k

To complete the ruse, I set my status to *In a meeting*. I needed time to think. There could only be one reason he was calling. I squeezed my eyes shut and massaged my forehead. Maybe he just wanted a friend, or a workout buddy, or a recommendation for a hairdresser . . . oops, whatever, didn't matter. If he asked me out again, I'd just say no. I was 55, somewhat successful, and SINGLE! I wasn't going to spend the rest of my life worrying about hurting some man's feelings, especially when I hadn't been given the same consideration.

I worked for another hour, then noticed he was online. Determined to get it over with, I pinged him.

Me: u there?

Bill: yeah can i call?

Me: sure

I picked up my cell and shut my cube door, then let the phone ring a few times before answering with a quiet, friendly, "Hello Bill, how are you?"

"Fine. Nice to hear your voice."

He talked in circles for a while before getting to the point.

"Was wondering if you were going to the company picnic at Rogers Park this evening."

I sighed.

"Yes, I go every year. I don't remember ever seeing you there."

"My wife and I used to go when they first started it. There wasn't much to do back then, but I hear it's grown into a really good time."

I wasn't interested in continuing the pointless exchange, so I responded with an unenthusiastic, "Yep."

"Can I pick you up?" he asked.

"No, I have a ride."

It came out like a slap, so I added, "But I can meet you at the bar."

I could almost hear him deflating.

"OK, see you there," he said weakly.

I touched the phone to hang up the call and considered how much less attractive Bill was as a wounded puppy. It would be easier than I first thought to stop thinking about him—especially since I wouldn't be watching him throwin' iron in the gym.

I was wearing the same outfit I had worn the year before—blue jeans and a chambray button-down shirt tied low over a white cami. It all still fit, thanks to Spandex. Technically, it was a company function, so I thought twice about the sexy balconette bra. I hadn't worn it since Lance left me and wasn't sure why I was wearing it now.

I thought of Doug the UPS guy delivering all the X-rated toys and clothes; I'm sure he knew what was in those unmarked boxes. But in the end, what had it all been for? My husband still left me for someone younger. TO BE CLEAR, this girl was not smarter, funnier, richer, or even better looking than me. All she was, was younger.

Fuck him!

DING-DONG!

I opened the door and there were my two young wingmen, Brian and Craig, right on time with a pre-party warm-up bottle of spiced honey tequila. I motioned for them to move to the patio where the bar was prepared with shot glasses, cut up limes, and sea salt.

The boys and I had been hired by SEA's Operations Division the same month and had become fast friends. Shortly thereafter, I became their supervisor, which was downright embarrassing, considering how much more they knew about day-to-day operations. But as it turned out, the job was a good fit, and Brian and Craig figured they'd be better off with me than someone they didn't know or trust.

I carried a plate of tortilla chips and some homemade guacamole out to the patio, placed it on the white wicker coffee table in front of them, and then casually asked, "So, do either of you know Bill Pruitt?"

"Nope. Should we?" they answered in unison.

"He's a guy I know from the gym. Just found out he works for SEA. He asked if he could take me to the picnic tonight."

Brian and Craig raised their eyebrows.

"I said no, because I always go with you guys."

"Hey man," Craig said, running his hand through his shaggy blond hair, "don't let us cramp your style."

"Not sure if he might ask to drive me home. You're my ride, right?" I said it as if it were a directive, and Craig knew I was serious.

"Um, OK," he said.

Brian's dark eyes darted back and forth between Craig and me, as if his sixth sense antennae had intercepted some inaudible signaling.

"This guy's not bothering you, is he?" Brian asked, sounding more like a big brother.

I waved him off.

"No, no . . . he's just . . . he's lonely."

Craig was about to shove a chip in his mouth, but stopped and looked at me like a curious child.

"Are you lonely?"

"Sometimes," I said, sipping some tequila from the edge of the shot glass.

The boys were looking at me intently, waiting for me to expand on my one word response to Craig's very personal question.

"Look, I've been married most of my life and it didn't work out the way I expected. I'm not interested in doing it again, and I don't want to lead this guy on. What about you two?" I asked, bunting the ball back into their court, then downing the rest of the shot.

Brian harrumphed. "Screw that. I'm still paying for my first mistake."

Craig squeezed his thumb and index finger together and squinted. "Missed it by that much." He grinned and then added, "I don't know, maybe when I'm 50."

"And she'll be 30, right?" I asked, with a hearty dose of sarcasm.

"Not even," Craig said, grinning ear-to-ear, completely unaware that his endorsement of the trophy wife stereotype had hit a sore spot. But Brian noticed. He poured us a final one, then he put his arm around my shoulder and squeezed it.

"Listen, Sally," he said, "no matter what happens tonight, we've got your back."

CHAPTER THREE

Awesome Van

Rogers Park is a stunning 400-acre preserve with a campground, trails, and a community center; a perfect venue for a company as large as SEA. Orange-vested parking volunteers were directing traffic as we rolled in with the crowd. The DJ was playing "Pontoon," a crowd favorite around here where boats are bountiful. I could smell barbeque and other food truck fare, and I couldn't wait for that first cold one.

Brian parked and we walked through the field heading for the bar. Craig hung back and fired up his vaping device. He was trying to quit smoking, and I wished him well. I never cared much for smoking myself. I medicate with alcohol.

The mobile pub was actually a very long trailer, the sides of which flipped up to reveal 20 taps of various craft drafts, as well as the necessary bartenders to pull and pour. It was shiny black with the Guinness name and logo across the top and had a spiral staircase leading to the trailer rooftop, providing a better view of the festivities. Brian and I cozied up to the bar near the Green Flash taps and ordered the West Coast IPA, and then I saw him.

What a doof.

Bill was sporting a nondescript long-sleeve beige button-down shirt, presumably purchased from Pedophiles-R-Us. It was tucked into old Levis, the jean's hem not quite long enough to reach his flip flops. He might have been able to get away with the ensemble if he hadn't opted to accessorize with a cowboy hat. The only thing that could have made it worse would have been mandals. He was shaking hands and slapping backs, having a gay old time.

I elbowed Brian.

"That's Bill there . . . in the hat."

Before Brian could respond, Bill saw me, waved, and was seemingly transported at the speed of light to our location.

"Hey, you made it," he said.

"Yeah . . . hi . . . ah . . . this is my friend, Brian."

Bill shook Brian's hand vigorously. He was obviously in a good mood, and I wondered if he, like me, had hit the sauce before arriving—that would at least help to explain the outfit.

"And this is Craig," I said.

Bill latched onto Craig's hand just as Craig got to the bar and shook it like they were good friends who hadn't seen each other in a few years.

Bill turned to me, placed his hand gingerly on my arm, and looked mysteriously into my eyes.

"Can I show you something?" he asked.

"Sure, what?" I said, almost expecting him to pull a quarter from behind my ear.

"MY . . . NEW . . . VAN! It's totally pimped out!"

So, the guy I had been lusting after was really a Gomer.

This is why they call it fantasy.

I took a deep breath.

"Ahhh, sure where is it?"

"It's out in the field pretty far," he answered, prancing around like a Lipizzaner stallion.

"All right, let's go," I said, anxious to get this guy away from Brian and Craig and anyone else I knew.

Bill took me by the hand and started pulling me towards the domain of vehicles. I turned around and mouthed a reassuring Be right back to the boys.

"That's it right there, that big orange one with the raised blue roof," Bill said with pride, pointing at the garish gas guzzler peppered with University of Florida insignia.

The fact that he was an Engineering Gator wasn't surprising as they are a dime a dozen at SEA. I'm one myself, enrolling at UF when my parents moved us from our little town in Ontario to the beaches of central Florida. I had planned to study English Lit at McGill University in Montreal or at Queen's University in Kingston, but once removed from that opportunity by sheer geography, I succumbed to the pressure from my father to "Do something with math."

Bill had his arms stretched out straight in front of him. His eyebrows were raised. He was holding his breath, waiting for my reaction.

"So you're a Gator," I said, stating the obvious.

"Go Gators!" he said with an enthusiastic exhale, slapping his palms together and doing the Gator chomp.

"I am too," I said, much subdued.

"No kidding!" he said excitedly, and I thought I detected a whiff of bullshit.

Bill pressed a button on his key fob and the over-sized side door skated open.

Holy cow! It WAS pimped out.

He jumped in, threw his hat on the bed, and held out his hand. I took it and he pulled me in with such force, we banged into some cabinets.

"Oops," he said with a chuckle. "Sorry about that."

Without the hat on, Bill could stand up without hitting his head. I remembered my mother and grandmother saying it was bad luck to put a hat on the bed. That's silly superstition of course, but I picked it up anyway. It was sweaty.

I turned my focus to the van and stepped around in a slow circle, nodding, taking it all in. It had that new van smell which, not surprisingly, is the same as that new car smell.

Bill described everything like an animated used-car salesman: the burl wood paneling on the dash, the state of the art electronics, the soft, cobalt-colored leather seats, the spinning, reclining captain's chairs, the 32-inch flat panel TV, the tiny but very functional kitchenette, and the obligatory moon roof pitched 45 degrees, letting the fresh air in. And in the back, no surprise, a queen-sized bed. My dad had a tricked out van—nothing as grand as Bill's, of course—but the setup was somewhat familiar.

"I'm guessing the bed converts to a table and bench seating," I said.

"Sure does, but I leave it made up as a bed. It's really comfy, want to try it out?"

This time, the scent of bullshit was unmistakable.

"You're screwing with me, aren't you, Bill?"

"What do you mean?" he asked, playing the idiot.

"You sound different, you're acting different, you're wearing this stupid cowboy hat."

I threw the hat on a captain's chair.

"That's not a hat, that's a Stetson, and how do you know who I am or how I should be acting?"

The Gomer was gone.

"You really don't know me at all," he said. "At lunch I told you about my wife and how much I missed her, and that I wanted to find someone special to spend the rest of my life with. After that, I couldn't get a word in edgewise. I listened to your long-winded woe-is-me tale that ended with your great declaration: you just want to get laid. I think it was you who was screwing with me."

That was unexpected.

"I guess I got carried away," I said, shrugging, feeling no need to apologize.

I sat down on a captain's chair and Bill perched on the bed.

"I like writing and telling stories, and of course I exaggerate to make a point, or to make the story more interesting."

I waited for a response, but Bill appeared to be waiting for something as well.

"Everything I told you was true, Bill. If I just said I was divorced, wouldn't you have asked for the details anyway?"

Bill didn't respond. He was still waiting. So I added, "I apologize if I didn't acknowledge your feelings and if I sounded crude. I'm truly sorry about the loss of your wife."

He looked down and started winding his watch before speaking.

"So, when you said you would never be monogamous again, you were exaggerating."

Hesitation.

"No. I wasn't exaggerating about that."

Bill looked up and then challenged my assertion.

"Then why did you grab my arms and pull me to you when I kissed your cheek?"

"Well, why did you kiss my cheek?" I popped up to standing, now on the offensive, which is more my style.

"Look, it's been a while. I'm sure if any other attractive man kissed my cheek, I would have done the same. Besides, I'm too old for you, we work at the same company, and I'm not interested in pair-bonding!"

I did the air quotes around pair-bonding for proper emphasis of the 17-point word.

"That's three good reasons this isn't going anywhere. Plus, that hat looks ridiculous on you."

I pointed to the hat, grinning a little, trying to break the tension.

Bill grinned a reluctant grin in response.

"My head will get sunburned if I don't wear a hat. How about this one?"

He opened a cabinet above the sink, grabbed a red baseball cap and put it on. It read: *I'm staging an epic comeback*.

"That's worse," I said, "and the sun's not out." He took it off. "And please untuck that shirt."

"I have another shirt."

He opened the narrow closet beside the fridge. Inside were shirts, pants, and nice leather shoes. He held up a tropical print, short-sleeved button-down.

I nodded approvingly.

"Yeah, that'll work, and those shoes are perfect."

Bill kicked his flip flops into the closet, grabbed the leather slip-ons, and sat back on the bed to put them on. He looked up and smiled at me, then stood and started unbuttoning the pedophile shirt.

It was awkward as I watched him take his shirt off, because he watched me watching him, but I refused to look away. I had waited this long to see his chest and damn it, I was going to SEE . . . HIS . . . CHEST!

It was just like I imagined—smooth, hairless, very tanned, broad, and muscular. I had the sudden urge to take my own shirt off and press my bare bazongas against his.

"Well, how do I look?" he asked as he finished buttoning up, his direct question snapping me out of my salacious stupor.

"Much better." I cleared my throat. "How about those tan pants?"

I pointed to the closet, trying to divert attention from myself. Bill started to unzip his jeans, then looked at me and stopped, out of modesty I guessed, so I turned my back to him.

Less than a minute later, I heard him say, "All done," and I turned to face him. He looked exactly like he did when we had lunch the week before. I smiled and nodded.

"Very handsome. Now, what are you going to say if someone asks you why you changed your clothes?"

"I'll say I was hot," he said and winked.

You are hot, I mused.

I was sure by now Bill had felt the intensity of my gaze, and by extension, my thoughts. He stepped towards me and put his hands on my shoulders and brushed his mouth against my ear.

"Sally, I'm going to kiss you again, on the lips this time," he murmured.

I stiffened.

Then he quickly, but barely, touched my lips with his. I felt that same electrostatic tingling. He broke away and looked into my eyes while gently stroking my lower lip with his thumb. Then he moved his fingers up the back of my neck, cradled my head in his hand, and rested his forehead against mine.

I thought it was over, so I opened my mouth to speak, but he kissed me again, harder, and with lips parted. He was breathing into me, teasing my lips with his tongue. I wrapped my arms around his neck and relaxed, inviting more of the same as his arm circled around my back and he slowly pulled me to him. He danced me backwards towards the bed, moving his lips across my cheek. When he nipped my neck, a bolt of lightning shot from his mouth through me to my center.

And then . . . voices. A family was getting into the truck next to Bill's van. I stopped feeling and starting thinking. I put my hands on Bill's chest and pushed back, my forehead knitted with concern.

"I need to get back to the party," I whispered.

Bill shook his head, keeping his arm firmly around my waist. "Not until you tell me any guy could make you feel what you just felt."

"What are you talking about?" I pushed him back harder until he let go and we were standing a few feet apart.

"You said you hadn't been with a man in a long time, and ANY guy could turn you on—that's why you grabbed my arms in the Clams' parking lot. I don't believe it."

I rolled my eyes.

"I'll have to get back to you on that, Bill. Right this second, I don't have anyone to compare you to, but rest assured, I'm working on it."

Bill crossed his arms. I could tell he didn't like the implication.

"I'm going back to the bar before Brian and Craig form a search party. Please be so kind as to give me a ten minute head start. Oh, and by the way . . . awesome van."

CHAPTER FOUR

Detroit Cinderella 99

I poked my head out of the van and looked both ways, like a cop about to enter a hallway of unknowns. Coming towards me were throngs of weary parents, pushing, carrying, and dragging their children and the various sundries required to care for them. I jumped out with my back to them and headed into the ocean of vehicles and a row of trees separating the park from the campground. As I hiked across the grass, my mind drifted to that make-out scene in Bill's van. Chemistry, electricity, biology—he had all the hard sciences working for him. Still, I was glad our intimacy had been interrupted. Bill's romantic notions were misplaced where I was concerned. I was passionate but not sentimental; I couldn't give him what he needed. And the fact that he worked for SEA just complicated the situation.

"Hey Sally!"

I spun around towards the loud whisper. It was dark and I don't see well at night, but luckily there was a full moon and the sky was alight with stars. I saw a hand wave and then made out two figures standing beside a van, one very tall with a beanpole frame, the other much shorter and rounder.

"Who goes there?" I whispered, but was almost up on them. The short one was my boss. I didn't know the tall one; he opened the side door of the van.

"Hi Mark," I said.

"Get in," he said, motioning with his hand, and out of habit, I did what he said. He entered behind me, and the stranger crawled in on his knees behind Mark. I sat down in a captain's chair and thought, Holy moley, it's déjà vu all over again. The stranger shut the door and lit a candle.

"This is my friend Jerry from Michigan," Mark said, sitting in the chair next to mine. I nodded, and Jerry nodded back as he sat down on the rug cross-legged. He reached into his shirt pocket, pulled out a joint, put the whole thing in his mouth to wet it, and then drew it out slowly until it rested down off his lower lip. Then he struggled to extricate a BIC from his jeans pocket and lit the joint, drawing hard until the end was on fire. He had a Unabomber beard, the kind that's popular with Unix programmers, and

I thought it might burst into flames. He passed the joint to Mark. I wasn't sure how to proceed.

"What about SEA's no drugs policy?" I asked.

"I've worked at SEA for almost 20 years," Mark said. He sucked hard on the joint, pulling in a lot of air, making a lot of noise, and then holding his breath for a few seconds before squeaking out the rest of the sentence.

"No one has ever been tested for drugs after the initial hiring. So here, enjoy our Detroit Cinderella 99."

At least that's what I thought he said. If squirrels could talk, I imagine that's how they'd sound. I reached for the joint and nervously took a small hit. I couldn't remember the last time I smoked pot or who with—damn sure it wasn't with my boss.

"Let's sit at the table," Mark said, getting up and sliding into a bench seat at the back of the van. Jerry slid in next to him. I sat opposite and looked around. The bizarreness of being in a second pimped out van in one night wasn't lost on me.

My turn again. This time I drew in hard.

Man, this is good shit.

I'm not sure if I said that out loud or if I just thought it.

"So, Sally," Mark said, "how well do you know Bill Pruitt?"

I hid my surprise at Mark's unexpected question and passed the joint to Jerry.

"Not well," I said. "He works out at my gym. I know he's a SEA engineer at Riverview. That's about it."

I hoped Mark was stoned, or that I was a really good actress.

Just kidding, I'm a fantastic actress.

Jerry passed the joint to Mark, who took another long hit and then did three quick tokes just to cram as much into his lungs as he could. I waited for him to explode. He looked up at me and then he did, coughing out a copious cloud. Ready for it, I pushed back against the seat and pulled my head in like a turtle.

"Well, he might have an engineering degree," Mark said, choking, "but he's a lawyer—a Level 6."

Curious omission.

Mark passed the burning stub to me. This thing was going to make the rounds about two more times before burning someone's fingers.

"Did he tell you his wife died a couple years ago?"

"Yes, he did," I said. "Very sad."

I took another long draw.

"Did he tell you anything else?"

"No," I said, remembering Bill's admonition that I hadn't given him the chance to say diddly squat.

Jerry was quietly nodding and rocking back and forth like he was listening to music, except the DJ had stopped spinning. I considered him more closely as I handed the joint over and watched him suck the last bit of life out of it. He needed a nickname. Seinfeld? No, definitely not; he was the opposite of Jerry Seinfeld. How about Mungo Jerry? He sort of looked like that guy in Mungo Jerry.

Remember their big hit? "In the summertime, when the weather is hot."

Our eyes met and he smiled at me. I smiled back. He was acceptable to me now because of that great song he wrote.

For some unknown reason, Mark was still talking about Bill.

"Well, apparently Pruitt was pretty shaken up about it. He became fixated on his administrative assistant, Jane Yarburg. You won't know her, she doesn't work for SEA anymore. She filed a sexual harassment claim against him."

Mark took a hit off of what looked like nothing.

Wait, WHAT did he just SAY?!

I struggled to remain calm.

"Well, obviously he didn't do it or he would have been fired, right? And what does this have to do with me, Mark? I barely know the guy."

I protested just a little too much, but I understood this fourth reason not to get involved with Pruitt was THE reason.

I shook my head at the offer of another hit. Mark offered the nothing to Mungo Jerry, and Jerry pinched the nothing from him. Surreal.

"Not only wasn't he fired," Mark said, "but within a few months, he got a fat promotion. The charge against him was dropped. Rumor has it, Jane was paid off. That's the way the world works—the rules are different for the rich and powerful."

"Are you suggesting Bill is rich and powerful?" I asked, puzzled by the direction the conversation had taken.

"You don't know this guy at all, do you?" Mark said. "His dad, who is dead now, was SEN . . . A . . . TOR Pruitt. His mom is still living, her brother was GOV . . . ER . . . NOR Leach." Mark exaggerated the political titles. "The family has shit tons of money and an impressive property on the ocean in Sundown Beach."

"Do you have any water?" I asked, feeling myself swing hard into a state of super-stonedness. Just then, I heard a couple of guitar chords. It was the band, cranking up their first set with 'Jumpin' Jack Flash."

"Oh shit, Mark. Can I use your phone?" I grabbed for it. "Do you have Brian's number?"

"Winslet? Yeah." Mark touched the screen a few times and handed it to me. It was ringing. Brian answered.

"Hi Mark."

"It's me, Sally."

"WHERE THE HELL ARE YOU?!!!" Brian bellowed.

"Well, obviously I'm with Mark! I'm sorry, I lost track of time."

"Bill came back to the bar 45 minutes ago wearing completely different clothes. We thought he murdered you and then changed clothes to cover up the blood spatter!"

"BAHAHAHAHAHAHA!!! That's absurd!" I said, unable to contain myself. "I'll be . . . hehehe . . . I'll be . . . hehehe. . . there in five minutes."

I hung up Mark's phone and handed it back to him.

"Thanks so much for the Cinderella 99, or whatever you called it," I said, giggling. "And so nice meeting you, Mungo Jerry."

Jerry looked confused by his new moniker. He opened the van door to let me out.

I jumped, landed, wobbled, and put one foot behind me to keep myself from falling over. Then I stepped together, arched my back, and threw my hands in the air like an Olympic gymnast who had just saved a good score. I stumbled towards the lights and sounds, trying not to step in a hole or doggy-do.

CHAPTER FIVE

Dirty Dancing

By the time I found my way back to the bar, my tongue was swollen and glued to the roof of my mouth. I pushed through the crowd with the occasional "sorry" and finally managed to get a cold craft draft in my hand. I sucked down half on the spot, then I saw the boys and shoved my way over to them.

"Hey dudes, any sign of Bill the axe murderer?" I winked and hiccuped simultaneously.

"He's been keeping an eye on us from the other side of the bar," said Craig, not amused. "I think he's been waiting for you to show up."

When Bill came around to join us, I just couldn't help myself.

"BILL! You changed your CLOTHES!"

"I was hot," Bill said, right on cue, but he was deadpan in his delivery. "What are you drinking?"

"Jalapeno Scul . . . no . . . no . . . no . . . no . . . that's not it . . . HabanENO . . . no . . . HabanERO Scuffin . . . no . . . Sculpin!" I struggled. "Want a sip?"

He raised his hand in a stop motion.

"No thanks, I don't like spicy."

"Reason number five!!!"

I hoisted my beer in the air, sending some of it over the edge of the glass.

Brian and Craig looked at each other confused, but Bill knew exactly what I was referring to. When I tried to pussy-whip him into ordering a Bud Light, he looked annoyed.

And then out of the crowd, she appeared: silver hair cut very short and chic, porcelain skin, hot pink lipstick, a white lace dress, jean jacket, and gray cowboy boots. A real class act. She touched Bill's shoulder.

"Hi stranger."

He turned around and beamed.

"Jane! How wonderful to see you!"

They embraced.

Holy SHIT, I thought, THE Jane? Lawsuit Jane? I steeled myself for the inevitable introduction, but Bill looked over his shoulder at me and said, "Excuse us," and they walked off together, his arm around her shoulder, guiding her through the crowd.

Brian spoke first.

"What's going on, Sally?"

"Let's move, BOYYYZZZZ!" I said crossing my arms in front of me gangsta-style. "I want some SUDS!"

They followed me to the Funky Buddha taps. I was hungry, so naturally I ordered the Maple Bacon Coffee Porter. As soon as the beer was in my hand, I admitted I was high.

"Keep your voice down, Sally," Craig said. "This is a drug-free crowd. Where did you get the smoke?"

"I won't say," I replied, putting my finger to my lips, "but it was crazy good, and the guy who provided it also provided some interesting information about Bill."

I took a couple gulps of the beer, DEEEE . . . licious . . . then recounted Mark's tale without, of course, revealing his name. After all, he was their boss too.

"I think that woman who Bill just walked off with is Lawsuit Jane."

"Well they sure don't look like legal adversaries," said Craig with a self-satisfied snort, like he was impressed with his choice of words.

"What happened in the van?" asked Brian.

"Bill or Jerry's?" I responded.

"Who the hell is Jerry?!"

"Mungo Jerry . . . never mind. Nothing happened in the van. Bill and I are just friends."

"Come on, Sally," Brian said, elbowing me and almost toppling me over. "There's something between you two, a force of some kind. It's pretty obvious."

Craig pointed to the dancefloor.

"Maybe not anymore. Maybe now the force is with Jane."

I followed Craig's finger to the disco lights bouncing off Bill's shiny dome as he danced with Jane to "You Spin Me Round." Strangely, I felt a pang of jealousy.

"Well hell's bells," I said, not willing to reveal the unwelcome envy. "You gotta' admit, he's got some moves."

I winked at Craig and Brian and then looked back at the dancefloor. Bill wasn't taking up much real estate, just moving in place, rocking his hips to the beat, so, so sexy. Jane, on the other hand, was bringing it big time. HMMPF! Sexual harassment my assment.

"Let's get something to eat," Brian said, massaging the dark shadow on his chin. "I'm starving."

"Me too," said Craig. "Let's hit that dumpling truck. You got the munchies, Sally?"

"Kinda, but I'm not killing this buzz yet. I really want to dance, so hurry up. In the meantime, I'm going to throw one back."

Before Brian and Craig could talk me out of it, I took off towards the very far end of the bar and joined the line of millennials waiting for shots. I squinted, struggling to read the menu while awaiting my turn.

Hmmmmm, let's see . . . Buttery Nipple, Panty Man, Kick in the Balls, Mind Eraser, Motor Oil, Hot Damn, Pineapple Upside Down Cake, B-52, White Gummy Bear, Absolut Bitch, Absolut Legspreader, Alice in Wonderland, Jolly Rancher, Irish Car Bomb, Partybar Schuffel, A Kick in the Crotch . . .

And then it was my turn to order.

"Ahhhh, just give me a shot of Patron," I handed the bartender a tenner, "and keep the change." He was pretty cute so I winked at him. He winked back. He knew what side his butt was breaded on, hehehe.

I jerked my head back and got almost all of the shot in my mouth. I swallowed and felt the heat spread through my body, then I slammed the empty shot glass on the bar like Clint Eastwood in a Spaghetti Western. I turned around and walked into him.

"Oops, sorry Bill." I chuckled, wiping my chin with the back of my hand. "Are you in line?"

"Ah, no . . . I just wondered if you would like to sit down for a minute. Can I get you something else?"

"No," I said, looking up at him flirtatiously. "I wanna dance."

I grabbed Bill's hand and dragged him back out on the dancefloor. The band was playing "Funky Town." Somewhat reluctantly, he began his reserved and arousing pelvic rock while I moved my hips in an exaggerated circle, twisting my arms in the air and backing up against him like a 10-dollar . . . no . . . 20-dollar hooker. Suck it, Jane, I thought, and imagined her appropriate response. No, YOU suck it, Sally!

BAHAHAHAHAHA! That is so funny.

Then the song was over, and just like in the movies, a slow one took its place. It was Al Green singing "Let's Stay Together." But Bill had been unphased by my indisputable skills, so I figured it was time to toss back another shot of Patron and find a more receptive partner. I mouthed an apathetic "thanks" and started to walk away, but he reached for my hand.

"One more, Sally?"

"Sure," I said, like I was doing him a favor.

We started in formal position: his right hand on my back, and my left hand on his shoulder, my other hand in his. Very soon into it, he started to loosen up and smile. Clearly, this music was more to his liking.

I moved my hand from his shoulder to the back of his neck and teased it a little with my fingers, and he pulled me in just a little closer and interlaced his fingers with mine. I drew our hands down until they rested between us. I wondered if Jane was watching.

Impaired as I was and pressed up against him, it was impossible to fight the frisky in me. I swiped my right index finger left to right across his nipple, then I looked up at him for a response, but he was peering down at me with no expression. So I did it again, just to make sure he knew it wasn't accidental. He pulled me in even tighter, and I flattened my cheek against his chest and dizzied with his red-blooded bouquet.

I let my left arm make way down his back, slowly tracing his spine with my thumbnail until my fingertips reached the bottom of his shirt. Then I slid my hand up under the shirt, pausing to rest my palm on his warm, bare back before angling my fingers beneath the waistband of his pants. I gazed up at him then closed my eyes. I wanted him to kiss me.

I felt a tap on my shoulder.

"Hey Sally, we're heading out."

It was Brian. He could tell by the expression on my face that I wanted to punch him in HIS.

"I can take you home," Bill offered, but Brian was glaring at me wide-eyed, and in a moment of clarity, I realized that he was only doing what he had promised to do. Plus, what would it look like if I left with Bill, especially considering my condition and what Mark had revealed.

"That's OK, Bill," I said unhappily, stepping back from him. "All my stuff is in Brian's truck and he drives right by my house. Thanks for the dance, though."

I flexed my wrist in a small wave and Brian reached for my arm and began to guide me away from my disappointed dance mate. When we got to our destination, Craig was leaning on Brian's truck, vaping.

"You know you're going to feel like shit tomorrow, right?" Craig said, talking through a puff of lavender mint.

"I'll be OK," I said, "I just need some food. Hey Brian, go through a drive-thru so I can get a burger."

Brian opened the truck door and I climbed in sloppily.

"That's not what he meant," Brian said. "He means you're going to feel badly about your behavior."

I swallowed that anxious voice that typically doesn't make itself heard until the morning after —the one that asks, Did I say or do something inappropriate?

Craig was beside me in the truck now, and Brian was in a line of cars waiting to pull out onto the highway.

"We don't want to make it sound more serious than it was," Craig said, noticing my agitation, "but obviously you had a little too much tonight. I'm sure everyone thinks you were just having a good time but—"

"But what?" I asked, afraid of the answer.

A moment of silence.

"Well," said Brian, "at the bar you were pretty loud, taunting Bill, and then the dancing . . . That was over the top."

I was starting to feel sick.

"What about it?"

"You were on him like white on rice," explained Craig, plainly. "That's why we decided to leave, and why Brian interrupted you."

"So what?" I asked, trying to convince myself it was no big deal. "People touch each other when they're slow dancing."

"Oh really?" asked Brian. "You had your hands under his clothes! The poor guy looked nervous."

"Oh my God. I didn't think anyone was paying attention," I said, placing my head in my hands and hyperventilating.

"It's OK," said Craig, patting my shoulder. "We just wanted to get you out of there before it escalated." Then he added, "I thought you said you didn't want to lead this guy on."

I didn't respond and the talking stopped. I motioned to Brian to roll down the windows because I was nauseous. We finally got to my house and I fought to get out of the truck, still very impaired.

"You gonna be all right?" Brian asked.

"Yeah. And sorry. I'm old enough to know better."

"Look on the bright side," Craig said. "This evening has served up one helluva story. Do you have any idea what you're going to call it?"

But of course I did.

"Dirty Dancing."

I never got that burger, so I was hungry, but more than that, I was confused. There was no denying Bill could light a fire in me, but I'd made it abundantly clear that heat was all I was interested in. Why then did I get jealous when he left me to spend time with Lawsuit Jane? While I was pondering this great mystery, I fought to get out of my clothes. After finally wrestling my cowboy boots off, I barely got one leg out of my jeans before I stumbled and hit my head on the dresser.

DAMN IT!

And so the next morning, as one might expect, I did feel like shit. Head pounding, I called him.

"Good morning," he answered cheerfully.

"Hi Bill."

"How are you?"

"Not good."

And then in the background, "More coffee, Bill?"

I wondered if it was Jane.

"Hey, I'm sorry to interrupt. You've got company."

"No, no, that's OK," Bill said, "I'll just step outside."

I heard the swish . . . swish . . . of a sliding glass door, and then Bill continued, apparently happy I had called.

"I figured something really interesting must have happened between the time you left my van and the time you returned to the bar. Not that what happened in the van wasn't inter—"

"Bill, I'm calling to apologize," I said, cutting him off. "I don't remember much after your van, but my friends said I was rude to you. And my antics on the dancefloor probably ruined both our reputations."

Bill chuckled. "If it's any consolation, mine was already ruined."

"Well, thanks for being so understanding. That's all I called to say. Have a great rest of your weekend."

"Wait . . . ah . . . by any chance are you going to Orlando Retreat Week at the Grand Tropics?" Bill interjected.

"Yes. My boss is presenting Wednesday morning."

"I'm presenting Thursday afternoon," he said. "Just going up for that last night. Maybe we can talk more then?"

"Sure," I said, although it sounded non-committal. "Talk to you later."

"All right, Sally, thanks for calling."

And so once again, things with Bill were left unresolved. I considered our relationship in terms of a Venn diagram. In his circle were stability, conventionality, and commitment. In mine were independence, inappropriate behavior, and hopefully soon, friends-with-benefits. Our circles did intersect, but only on one shared parameter: pronounced sexual attraction to each other. If only that was enough to negate all the reasons not to get involved with him.

CHAPTER SIX

The Orlando Schtupp

Over an hour had passed since I left Bill at the Slice & Hook bar at the Grand Tropics Hotel in Orlando. He hadn't texted or called, so I figured he had plenty of company. His presentation that afternoon had been captivating, not the typical PowerPoint offering—he didn't need props. He was a great speaker: charming, funny, and obviously quite knowledgeable. I imagined he was surrounded by other attendees, introducing themselves and asking questions.

I stood and swayed, the two gin and sodas at the bar, and two glasses of Sauvignon Blanc on the couch making themselves known. This was a good thing. One less or one more would have made a trip back down to the festivities far more likely, increasing the risk of a verbal or physical misstep—highly inadvisable, especially so soon after my performance at Rogers Park. The Monday after my dubious dancing debut, some inquiring minds had asked if I'd "recovered." I laughed it off, saying I shouldn't have skipped dinner, but I have a bad habit of teasing that line between appropriate and inappropriate behavior, and clearly I had tripped over it that night.

I pulled the dress over my head and fought my way out of my Spanx, then reached for my housecoat and noticed the tag . . . Comfy Janes. Ironic. My threadbare housecoat had the same name as Bill's old obsession. This was an obvious nicknaming opportunity. It was official. Lawsuit Jane would henceforth be known as Comfy Jane. I put her on, snapped her up, and looked around for my traveling wine bag.

Ah yes, Sebastiani Cabernet Sauvignon. An old standard, and a perfect pairing with a juicy burger. Unfortunately, it took me five minutes to wrestle the cork out, splashing ruby red onto the neckline of my Comfy Janes and complimenting the spaghetti sauce from the previous evening.

Why aren't all wines on the screw-off cap standard?

I poured a half glass and picked up the hotel phone to call room service, but my cell rang. It was Bill.

"Hi," I said.

"Hey, you coming back down . . . for dinner?"

"No, I'm in for the night. I'm going to order room service."

"Waaannnt some company?" he asked. He sounded a little tipsy.

"Well, I'm ready for bed."

"I'm hungry too . . . and . . . um . . . we haven't really talked seriously since Rogers Park. How about a pajama party?"

Talk seriously? Is that code?

I took a big swig of Cab and decided to play along.

"Pajama party. Hmmmm. How do you plan on getting to my room in your PJs without someone seeing you?"

"Through the adjoining room door," Bill replied, somewhat sheepishly.

"You changed rooms?!" I said, surprised by this tactical move, evidently made right after I'd left the bar.

Bill didn't respond.

"Geez, Bill, you're really putting me on the spot here," I said, as I turned to look at the bolted adjoining room door. I imagined him sneaking through it in his PJs to *talk seriously*, then disappearing with no one being the wiser.

It should have been a firm no, but I answered: "Ummmm, OK I guess . . . give me 20 minutes."

"Knock when you're ready," Bill said, his voice now revised from its former jolly tenor to a low, desirous purr. My heart did some triple time in response. I put down my wine glass and started running the bath.

I surveyed the room: definitely not ready for company. The sitting area was cluttered with hotel and company-related paper. I gathered it up and stuffed it into my case. The balcony was tidy, but it was almost dark, so the view would be limited, and possibly our voices would be heard out there. I shut the sliding glass door and drew the curtains. I picked up my dirty clothes and threw them into the closet then smoothed the duvet on the king-sized bed.

Like most people my age, I'm more attractive in low light, so I turned on the desk and floor lamps and turned off the overheads. Still, something was missing. Music. I started up my smooth jazz playlist and adjusted the volume down, in the unlikely event there would be any actual talking.

Why was I going to all this trouble?

OOOH! AHHH! OOOH! AHHH! I lowered myself into the hot water and splashed it up and around my neck and under my arms, then eased back slowly and considered this man I had just invited into my hotel room in his pajamas.

Sexual harassment is a serious charge that does serious damage, even if it's eventually proven to be untrue. Bill wasn't fired; he was promoted. Still, my boss was suspicious of him. There was no denying that despite his gentlemanly disposition, Bill wasn't shy when it came to women. The surprising full-body contact and ass grab in the Clams parking lot, the passionate kiss he demanded at Rogers Park, and now this calculated room re-positioning—it all gave testament to his boldness. But Bill wasn't a player. His spirited tactical maneuvers were part of a long-term connubial strategy, and his sights were laser focused, first on her and now on me.

And who was this Comfy Jane anyway? Was she the kind of woman who would file suit against an innocent man then start churning butter with him? At the very least, she and Bill were close friends; it made no sense. This confusion was just another reason to keep him at arm's length. Problem was I wanted more of what he showed me in his van, and I guessed he knew it.

Donning my Comfy Janes once again, I turned to the mirror and instantly deflated. The housecoat screamed "Let's play cards!" I had plenty of sexy lingerie at home, but of course I didn't bring any. And even if I had, I wouldn't wear it.

Fuckity, fuck, fuck, fuck!

KNOCK!

I jumped, then nervously opened the adjoining door a crack and peeked around the corner.

"You told me to knock when I was ready, Bill. Why are you knocking?"

He shrugged. "Guess I couldn't wait."

Like a soldier he stood—still, straight, and dressed neatly in his classic crisp navy blue pajama ensemble, the white-piped button-down top embroidered with WAP on the pocket in fancy font, no doubt a Christmas gift.

"What does the 'A' stand for?"

"Arthur . . . can I come in?" Bill asked, tentatively, as if unsure the offer was still good.

"Take off your shirt," I said, still hiding behind the door, and Bill puckered his brow with the strain of mental forces.

"This sounds familiar. You don't like what I'm wearing?"

"No, I don't like what I'M wearing. Please give me your shirt."

For the second time, I watched Bill remove his shirt while he watched me watch him.

"Let me grab a tee shirt," he said with some modesty, breaking from my lascivious stare.

"Give me five," I said, snatching the shirt as I shut the door on him.

SNAP! SNAP! SNAP! SNAP! SNAP!

I ripped open the housecoat and tossed it in the closet, then slipped into Bill's PJ top, rolling up the sleeves and buttoning it from the middle of the chest down. I returned to the mirror. The odds of organ grinding were now most certainly a certainty. I turned to gauge the view from the rear, and a memory from the day my marriage ended flashed in my head: that smirk on what's-her-name's face as she raked her long blonde hair into a ponytail, Lance's blue oxford shirt skating up her creamy, toned thighs.

Bill knocked again, bringing me back to the occasion, and I opened the door and walked awkwardly rearwards until I hit the backside of the large upholstered chair. I leaned back and crossed my legs, posing as if for the cover of *Senior Living* magazine and its feature article, "Yes, You Still CAN!"

Bill walked in, raised his eyebrows, smiled, and nodded approvingly.

"What were you wearing before?"

"An old housecoat."

"Then glad I could be of service."

Frozen about ten feet apart, we entered a staring

contest, which I promptly lost, feigning interest in my chipped toenail polish. We were supposed to be ordering room service, but the elephant in the room had to be fed first.

"Glass of wine?" I offered, raising my gaze.

"No thanks."

He was still staring, feet glued to the floor.

"Bill," I said, my voice shaking, "I'm afraid."

That thawed him and he approached, his hands ambling lightly down my arms, the sparks from the ignition of his touch snapping between my skin and the cool cotton shirt. He interlaced his fingers with mine, looked down into my eyes, and gently smiled.

"What are you afraid of?"

"I'm afraid I'm really going to like it."

Bill laughed and embraced me, and I complied without thought, my lips quivering, then softening under his, accepting his determined tongue, then answering with my own. I was ready for the familiar buzzing, then the shock through me to the apex of my legs, the swelling and the steamy dewfall. Would this reflexive response be the same in the arms of another?

His appetite aroused with my greedy reception, he kissed with increasing hunger and passion. I moved my head sideways and back to catch my breath, and he sailed his tongue back and forth along my collar-bone. Glorious tickle.

There was nowhere to go but more, and Bill wasted no time getting there. His hands stretched wide around my bare bottom, squeezing, then inching me up on the back of the chair. The chair tipped with my weight and Bill wrapped his arm around my waist to steady me. I wrapped my legs around his hips in response, pushing up into him, fighting to feel his flagpole through his pajamas. That was all the notice he needed. His lips fusing back onto mine, his fingers kneading my swollen breasts through the firm fabric, then fighting to unfasten the top button.

We were necking and dry humping like teenagers, his stiffening staff about to escape the confines of the PJ pants through the fly opening. Everything was happening so fast, I thought he might try to slay the vadragon right there against the chair. I pushed him back a little and slowly exhaled. He stepped away and took a deep breath himself, then reached for my hand and led me to the bed, his Swingin' Dick Nixon waving wildly in his pants.

I glanced at the clock and guessed it would all be over in about five minutes.

I sat on the end of the bed then scooted back, the slippery swelling between my legs ticking, ticking, like a time bomb. He followed over me, his eyes anchored into my own. Then he lowered himself and whispered words with such heart-stopping tenderness, it masked their pornographic essence:

"Spread your legs for me, Sally."

I did. And forgetting for a moment that I wasn't married, and this man who had just opened the Gates of Mordor wasn't Lance, I returned his whisper quite indelicately.

"Fuck me. I can't wait."

Bill rose up and looked at me, apparently surprised by my explicit phraseology.

Hey, he started it!

Ignoring my request, he rolled to my side and unfastened another button on the PJ top. This time there was no fumbling—he was calm, meticulous, and determined in his methods. His warm fingers skimmed into the open space and rippled over my pebbled nipples, brushing past and back, circling, pinching, torturing. The anticipation so agonizing, I went stiff.

"Relax," he said softly into my ear, his cool minty breath drifting along my charged flesh, the resonant bass tone he apparently reserved for times such as this provoking a contradictory response. I balled the bedding into my fists and pointed my toes.

"I've been dreaming of this night," he said, petting the inside of my damp quivery thigh with his warm palm, his fingers trailing in the wake of the current flowing behind it. When the heel of his hand discovered my hard kernel of tormented flesh, he pressed into it, while his fingers, one then another, introduced themselves before dancing inside of my flaming cave.

I writhed and rolled with pleasure, then feeling him grow thick against me, I curled towards him and slid my fingers under his waistband.

It was big. Not as big as I fantasized, of course—pretty sure that never happens—but it was still a good size. More importantly, it was hard, like a chain. I tugged on it, and then again, skin sliding inside of skin, and Bill responded to my unspoken urgency by rolling on top of me, working his legs between mine, then sweeping the curls from my face and brushing his lips against my mouth with unbearable lightness.

He raised himself to his knees and disrobed, exposing his robust, tanned, toned frame, and eager Excalibur. And then unexpectedly, he started stroking himself, his hooded eyes liquid with lust as they washed over my half nakedness. He appeared to be waiting for something, and so I joined him, sweeping my left hand to my breast and my right to my center, playing the petals with my piano fingers. Ten seconds into it, I started begging.

"Bill, please," I groaned. "I need this . . . you . . . so badly."

Oops.

He moved towards and against me, sweeping up and down across my covetous chasm, then centered himself on the target, teased me apart, and nudged in. As he lowered and slowly buried the rest of his length, he whispered my name.

"Oh . . . GOD . . . YES!" I yelled as his welcome invasion forced the words from the back of my throat. I wrapped his body with mine and hugged him to me like a drowning woman to a life raft in a raging storm. Negotiating that edge, I teetered on the brink of convulsion as I waited for him to catch up.

"It's so tight, so hot, like a volcano," he said, groaning into my ear, the end-of-day stubble on his chin another reminder of the maleness I'd so missed.

I turned my head to the left and caught us going at it in the mirrored closet door, and for a few seconds I detached from it, as if watching a movie, perfectly cast, perfectly directed, the mechanics excessively erotic. And then I became acutely aware that I was the image beneath the muscled chassis getting the piston put to me. The explosive between my legs was seconds from detonation.

Bill turned his possessive gaze to the mirror and we locked eyes by way of our reflection. When I mouthed the words "I'm coming," he read my lips and then unleashed the wildness brewing beneath his gentleness.

BANG! FUCK! SHOCK!

I soared through him and above him, riding a rush of tremors as the mighty spasm reached beyond its origin to claim my totality. My eyes rolled back into blackness as the words, "Oh FUCK that's good!!!" tore from my chest.

Trust me, I was trying to tone it down.

Bill watched himself in the mirror bringing me off, the raw visual triggering his release. He whispered something—I couldn't make out the words—then eyes squeezed shut, lips pinched, nostrils flaring like a racehorse driving to the finish line, he fell onto me, deeper into me, and shouted, "Oh . . . yeah . . . Sally . . . oh BABY!!" before flooding me with three final, deep, rough thrusts.

I glanced at the clock. Yep, five minutes.

And then, except for our breathing returning to normal, the world muted.

So I CAN do it, I thought, and now that I've done it, I can't wait to do it again. But this first time, The Orlando Schtupp, this would be remembered. This would be recounted.

CHAPTER SEVEN

No Condom

Bill found my hand and squeezed it tight, and I thought, uh oh, here's where he blows it with relationship talk. But he didn't.

"I'm starving," he said.

"Me too."

"Do you know what you want?" he asked

Of course I did, so I described it in detail: cheeseburger, medium, mustard, mayo, tomato, onion, and pickles—no lettuce—and fries, but only if they had gravy.

I could tell Bill was wishing he had pen and paper.

He started to get up and I saw his tanned bare back and just a flash of crack. Then he stopped abruptly, lay back down, and pulled the sheet over himself. He had been pretty demonstrative during the act itself but was now too modest to walk around naked in front of a lady, although he might have had a hard time categorizing me as such.

"I'm going to freshen up. Go ahead and order," I said.

I walked the short distance into the bathroom, locked the door, and unfastened the last few buttons of Bill's rumpled PJ top, allowing it to ease to the floor. The water in the shower sprayed hot from the rain head, steaming up the glass cage. I stepped in, closing the door behind me, and as I did, Bill's warmth trickled down my inner thigh. Ahhhhh, felt good. This manmade orgasm was a nice change from my handmade ones.

Wait, WHAT?! No condom! Shit! YES, we were in our 50's but so were all those STD-carriers living at The Villages! Who else had Bill been tromboning? Comfy Jane, I suspected. Doubtful she had cooties, but guessing he had slept with other women too and likely much younger.

I found Bill making himself at home on the couch, fidgeting with his phone. He looked up, winked at me and said, "Should be on its way," and I immediately felt a change in my attitude towards him.

It was awkward with him so relaxed, like this was his room, like we were a couple. I hoped the food arrived soon so I could wrap this up.

"I'm going to have a glass of red wine. Do you want one?" I asked, reaching for the bottle.

"No, I'm done," he said without looking up. "I'll grab some water when the food comes."

He obviously doesn't drink a lot, I mused, while pouring myself a half glass. Well, that was a point in his favor.

Marry a man who doesn't drink and you'll always have a designated driver.

KNOCK!

I didn't want anyone, not even room service, to know about the mattress dancing, so I hid in the bathroom. Bill opened the door and much to my distress, I heard Mark's confused voice.

"Is Sally here?"

Thankfully, Bill didn't miss a beat.

"Sally who?"

"Sally Shaw. You were talking to her at the bar this afternoon." Mark sounded suspicious.

"Oh yeah, Sally Shaw. No, she isn't here. Why would she be?"

"I thought she told me this was her room. I'm sorry. I've got her number. I'll call her again."

"No problem. Have a good evening."

"I'm Mark Martin, by the way. Sally's boss. That was a great presentation."

"Thanks, Mark. Nice to meet you."

I imagined them shaking hands.

"Have a good evening," Bill said again, and then I heard the door shut.

I flew out of the bathroom.

"Holy SHIT!" I said. I put my hands over my face, shaking my head as I talked through my fingers.

"Oh my God, Bill, this is exACTly the kind of thing I didn't want to happen!"

"Relax, honey. He just thinks he got a room number mixed up. It's no big deal."

Bill walked towards me, put his hands on my shoulders, and then pulled me in for a supportive hug. I didn't hug him back—and why was he calling me honey? Better question was, why was I surprised? Surely this was the kind of thing that happened to people dumb enough to bump bellies with their co-worker at a company retreat!

Where the HELL was that burger?

I broke away from him and moved to the front door, then looked around the room from what would have been Mark's vantage point. Thank goodness I had tidied up in preparation for Bill's arrival. There was really nothing to indicate it was my room, or that more than one person had been in it—no clothes lying around, no extra glasses, nothing girly. The adjoining door was open, but Mark wouldn't have been able to see it from this angle.

KNOCK!

Once again, I disappeared into the bathroom. It was room service. This was a teachable moment. Using my room as a base of operations for sex and supper had been a rookie mistake. Using his room would have solved the Mark problem, as well as the problem of getting Bill out of here. Lesson learned.

When I returned to the living area, Bill was placing a large silver tray on the dresser. I lifted one of the metal lids. What was this? A salad? This must be wrong.

"That's mine," Bill said, picking it up along with cutlery and a small carafe of ranch dressing. He sat down at the little table for two and looked at his meager feast with great anticipation, waiting, like a gentleman, for me to join him.

"Go ahead," I said with some sarcasm, "don't let it get cold."

I opened the other lid and there was my cheese-burger WITH fries AND gravy. I was barely in the chair when I took that first gigantic bite and grease ran down my chin. I picked up the miniature bowl of gravy and poured the hot brown marvelousness on the fries, then covered the fries with pepper. Bill was gnawing noisily on his greens like a ravenous rabbit.

"So Bill," I said, mouth half full, "first and fore-most, I want to say that was awesome sex."

I looked up at him nodding and smiling while savoring my burger. Bill nodded back unenthusiasti-cally, realizing the jiggery-pokery hadn't quite meant the same to me as it had to him.

"Is that what it was? Just sex?"

"Wellllll, obviously it was just sex," I said, rees-tablishing the rules. "But it was awesome just sex."

I did air quotes with my fingers around the just sex part of the sentence and grease ran down my arm. This time I caught it with a napkin. And then I broached the subject of the unprotected nature of the awesome sex.

"You didn't wear a condom."

He looked up, swallowed, and then wiped his mouth with his napkin, preparing for his defense. I filled a fork with gooey fries and shoved them in my mouth, waiting.

"You didn't say anything, and I figured you couldn't get pregnant so—"

BLAPP!

I slapped the table just hard enough to make the wine paint the inside of the glass, but not enough to tip the glass over. Bill furrowed his brows and pulled his head back in response.

"You do realize, Bill, there are other reasons to wear a rubber besides pregnancy, and how do you know I can't get pregnant?"

Why was I starting an argument?

"You're not serious, right? Look, you didn't say anything. You were faithfully married to the same guy for over 30 years, and I'm sure I'm fine, so—"

"What about Comfy Jane?" I said, blurting it without forethought.

Bill's eyes opened wide.

"COMfy Jane? What does she have to do with this?" he said, now provoked.

"I'm sorry, Bill," I said, realizing my mistake. "She has nothing to do with this. I was just thinking she might be . . . well . . . someone you are having a relationship with . . . plus . . . maybe . . . other women from the gym or . . ."

I just kept digging that hole, unable to wordsmith my way out of it. I winced. Bill put down his fork.

"First, I'm not going to talk about Jane, period, except to say she is a wonderful woman. Second, yes, I've had sex with a few other women. Third! In each case, I wore a condom!"

Bill's voice crescendo-ed with the numbers.

"And FOURTH! I DO have CONDOMS! I've got one in my wallet and a brand new box in my suitcase, just hoping I'd get this chance with you tonight. I would have worn a WETSUIT if you had asked!"

Another teachable moment. We ate in silence for a minute and I reflected on it. This was not the way to work a friends-with-benefits relationship. Going forward, there would be no more mentioning other women or men, and it would be a condom EVERY time!

"Bill, it's none of my business who you sleep with, and I shouldn't have brought this up. I could have asked you to wear a condom and I didn't. Please, let's just forget I said anything." I softened my demeanor even further and added, "Tonight was truly an unforgettable experience. I'll be smiling for a week."

I popped the last bite of the burger in my mouth, reached across the short space between us, and patted his forearm. He stared at me like he was trying to make up his mind whether or not to ask me something, and then he did.

"Guessing you aren't interested in spending the night together."

"No . . . sorry," I responded quietly.

Perhaps that was a little harsh, but I was relatively certain at this point that Bill was a pusher, and I was determined to avoid any scope creep in our relationship.

I stood up and started to clear the table, arranging the dishes on the tray to minimize their visual impact. Bill got up to open the door for me, but I couldn't risk anyone seeing me in the hall so I handed the tray to him, and he set it outside on the hallway floor. When he came back in, he managed a smile, then thanked me for a nice evening. He was so businesslike, I actually thought he might shake my hand. But he just walked through the adjoining door and closed it. I closed my side too and slid the bolt.

In bed, alone with my phone, I noticed the two messages from Mark and thought about returning his call, but instead I texted Bill.

Me: U asleep?

Bill: No

Me: Regrets?

Bill: No enjoyed it. Hope you did too

Me: Was amazing ;)

Bill: Just get the feeling I'm pressuring you

Me: I think we want different things

Bill: Yep goodnight

Me: Night

How was it Bill and I always ended on somewhat of a sour note? Just one more reason not to . . . whatever. I put my cell down on the night stand and it immediately rang.

"Hey, Sally, hope I didn't wake you."

"Hi Mark, no, I'm awake."

"Funny thing, I went looking for you tonight and ended up knocking on Bill Pruitt's door."

"That's weird," I said, holding my breath.

"Yeah. So, Jeff called me after he talked to you. Wanted to know if I would release you to go up there for a month or more and work on the project at the site."

"In Montreal?!"

Mark laughed. "Is that a yes or a no?"

"It's a big YES! When do I go?"

"A week from Sunday. Jody has the details—she'll make the arrangements."

"Thanks, Mark. This couldn't have come at a better time. I think this is just what's needed to get the project back on track."

"I agree. OK, see you back at the office."

I drummed the mattress with my feet in exuberance. This could be my big break, my time to shine! I would be working at Jeff's side for at least a month, and I'm so much more impressive in person. Surely this would enhance my opportunities at SEA. And Montreal: so cosmopolitan, so far away, and the perfect place to do it zipless—sex for its own sake, without emotional involvement, or any ulterior motive or consequences. A welcome departure from my first attempt at just sex.

And I knew just who to call.

CHAPTER EIGHT

Smokin' Hot Sex

That night in the hotel I tossed and turned, nervous I would run into Bill in the morning, and I wrestled with various alternatives to keep that from happening. When I woke for the fourth time at 3 am, I got up and started packing.

I tripped over Bill's PJ top lying on the floor and wondered what to do with it. If I took it with me, he might try to arrange a meeting to exchange it; if I hung it on his hotel room door handle, someone might take it. I picked up a pen and scribbled on a piece of Grand Tropics stationary:

Didn't want to wake you. I'll drop your pajama top in the mail.

I slid the unsigned note under his door and then realized I didn't have his home address. I'd have to send it through the interoffice mail.

At 3:45 a.m. I was in the car and on the road back to Sydney, and by 7 a.m. I was in my office. It was most everyone's regular Friday off; my favorite day to be at work. Unless there was some sort of emergency, I would be able to focus on the QuebecNet project uninterrupted. I was pretty sure I wouldn't be hearing from Bill as there was no reason for him to call me, and he had made it clear he wasn't happy with how our evening together had ended. I was glad to be moving on to Montreal: 1,500 marvelous miles away.

Focused on the task at hand and determined to hit it out of the park when I presented to Jeff and the gang, the 4:30 pop-up reminder on my computer screen came as an unwelcome interruption. That is until I remembered what it was for—I was due at the River House for happy hour. Four-thirty is late to start drinking on a Friday in Florida, and I hoped Laura was already there saving a seat at the bar.

The River House is an upscale restaurant on the Sydney marina, and on the busy weekends, they block the parking spaces with cones, forcing patrons to use the valet service. That works well for the golden-agers, but it slows down the coming-and-going for the rest of the ambulatory clientele. Plus, one has the additional burden of maintaining small bills to cover the tip. There is one bright spot though—the valets themselves.

"Nice dress, Sally," Matt said, smiling as he brushed against my backside on his way to the driver's seat. "I'll be here when you're ready," he said with a wink, amping his tip prospects.

"Thanks Matt," I replied business-like, not returning the flirtation. I only had two bucks on me.

I walked through the front door and squeezed past a gaggle of gray hairs who were waiting for an early bird dinner table, then I caught sight of Laura, her tall, slim upper torso silhouetted by the wall of glass and the water and sun behind it. My best friend for almost all of my life, Laura was as friendly as she was attractive: mid-length auburn hair, dark eyes, a straight smile, and a pronounced posterior that bounced beneath her blue jeans, her waist exceedingly small by comparison. She was alone at the bar, which was surprising. Typically, I had to displace a prospective suitor sitting on the saved empty seat next to her.

"Hi Laura," I said, giving her a hug before struggling to mount the bar stool. I leaned onto the bar and lifted up so Laura could drag the stool forward.

Short people got no reason to live.

"Welcome back, Sally," said Gil the bartender, placing my usual gin and soda in front of me. I smiled a thank you at him, then held up my glass and clinked it against Laura's. Behind her, the white sheets of the sailing class provided the postcard panorama that reassured all who had entered that moving to Florida was an inspired decision.

"Well, Sally?" Laura said with a wink, reminding me I had tipped her off to the donut glazing in Orlando. As far as telling stories goes, Laura has always been my biggest fan. She had come up with the idea to put them in writing shortly after Lance's devastating duplicity. I had shrugged off her original prescription of therapy. Writing is a lot cheaper and therapy enough, or maybe I just tell myself that.

Laura pushed her empty glass forward and held up two fingers in a peace sign at Gil, then pointed them down into her glass. I started chug-a-lugging my drink, anticipating the arrival of the second.

"So unbelievably hot," I said, grinning mischievously before launching into The Orlando Schtupp. I detailed the steamy experience in slo-mo, exaggerating as I typically do, detailing the topography of Bill's smooth, copper-colored frame, and every rock hard ridge of muscle rolling beneath his clean, fresh, unperfumed skin. As for Bill's skill, it was impossible to overstate it, and in the telling of it, I relived it, and I ached for one more shot at it. But despite the heart pounding ecstasy of those five minutes, my carnal adventure had come to a cheerless conclusion. Physically, it had been a happy ending, but Bill had screwed it up with unrealistic expectations.

Laura looked perturbed.

"You know, it's not unrealistic to want to spend the night with someone you've just been extremely intimate with, Sally. He's not a gigolo."

"I'd be better off with a gigolo," I said. "And who are you to talk? You've been shellacking Clint's canoe for years, but you always manage to make it back home alone. You're lucky he lives in Toronto and can't just swing by your house. Bill lives only four miles up the road. If I start this sleepover nonsense, before you know it he'll have moved in."

"Touché," she said, nodding introspectively. "Are you going to see him again?"

"No, I don't think so. I'm not calling him, that's for damn sure, and why would he call me?"

"Well maybe because you just had smokin' hot sex." Laura chased her sarcastic tone with the rest of her gin.

"Smokin' hot sex is enough for me, but it's just a means to an end for Bill. He's looking for a wife."

I downed the rest of my drink and held up my empty glass for a toast.

"Here's to smokin' hot sex!" I said, drawing the surprise of two silver-haired sailors across the bar. Laura raised her empty glass to them and then clinked it against mine.

The beginning of the week was more of a manic Monday than usual. I was consumed with my project scheduling strategy and the following Tuesday's presentation of it to the folks up in Montreal, plus I had hundreds of unanswered emails left over from the previous week in Orlando. By mid-afternoon Wednesday, I was burned out. I leaned back in my chair, put my feet up on the desk, and closed my eyes.

Curiously, thoughts of Bill invaded my attempts at solace. It struck me I knew practically nothing about him. How long was he married? What did his wife die of? Did he have any children? These were things most people knew about each other before they did the mystery dance.

And speaking of smokin' hot sex, how had a mild-mannered engineer like Bill mastered the art of adult naptime? His voltaic caress, his strong, encouraging hands, and the reach and reflection of his fingers, those words he whispered in that low, foreign, hypnotic purr, compelling me to beg. Then the angling into me, the rhythmic reconnaissance, the tidal tremors, the shatter. And finally, the predatory gaze right before the animal in him declared victory.

Is it hot in here or is it just me?

I grabbed my cell and sunglasses and down the stairs I went, out into the sun-filled parking lot. It was 78 degrees and I embraced the Florida weather, which would be perfect from now until June. I turned left and began walking briskly up the sidewalk along the one mile loop around the corporate campus. I breathed in the fresh air, clearing the cobwebs, and on the exhale, my cell buzzed. Bill's ears must have been burning.

"Well hi there," I answered, friendly, in case he was still pouting.

"Hey, Sally, sorry to bother you at work."

"That's OK. I'm outside taking a break," I said, wondering what the reason was for his call.

"Ah . . . OK great . . . so I'm calling for a few reasons . . . um . . . well . . . First, thanks so much for getting that PJ top back to me, although it's a good thing no one was in my office when I opened the package, hahaha."

"I didn't have your home add—"

"My mom bought me those pajamas for Christmas," Bill said, cutting me off, "and I wear them when I'm down at her place. She would definitely notice if half were missing. So, again, hahaha-ha, thanks for that."

I tried to say no problem, but once again he stepped on my attempt.

"And also . . . and I feel a little awkward asking this but . . . ah . . . was wondering if you could do me a huge favor . . . and if you can't, no worries . . . I don't want to pressure you . . . but . . . um . . . Mom's having her yearly Finally Fall party on Saturday. You know . . . ah . . . I've been taking quite a bit of ribbing these past years, always showing up to these types of events alone . . . and . . . well . . . you know . . . it bothers her, and she's getting really old . . . I know that sounds like an excuse but anyway, I would really like it if you would be my date . . . ok, wrong word maybe . . . but anyway, I would be eternally grateful if you would accompany me."

His ramblings floated above my own more important silent ones. Back and forth, yes and no, I wavered in my response to his uneven invitation. Stringing him along wasn't right. But as far as relationships went, I'd done the right thing my whole life. I didn't owe any man anything. This was me time, and the me wanted one more round of chesterfield rugby with Bill.

"Where does your mom live?" I asked, buying time, but I knew where.

He started up again, accelerating and raising pitch, his fragmented run-on sentence culminating in a hopeful squeak.

"Sundown Beach!–about 30 minutes south–faster to go US 1–then back to the beach–over the Palm Causeway–you can stay in the carriage house!–totally private–you won't have to drive home–after a night of too much fun!!"

A good time and very possibly a great story: impossible to resist. I would be on my way to Montreal very early the next morning, but if I told him that, it would at the very least curb his enthusiasm.

"I guess I could do that for you," I said amiably.

"Thanks, Sally," he said, relieved he'd made the sale. "I really appreciate it, and I know you're going to have a great time. It's a pretty big affair, lots of good people, great food and drink, and even a live band Mom hires every year. It's not formal, although most of the women wear dresses. Anyway, I know you'll look great, no matter what you wear."

He paused before continuing, and I imagined him blushing.

"If you get there around five, you'll have some time to relax before the party. We could talk . . ."

I breathed in deep and raised my eyes to the sky, hoping I wasn't on my way to an unforced error.

"All right, send me the particulars and I'll be there about five."

He jumped in hurriedly. "OK, I'll email you the info right now." And then calmer and more deliberate, "It's so great to hear your voice, Sally. I can't wait to see you again."

"OK, bye Bill."

I hung up and considered what I had set in motion yet again. Just five days ago at the River House, I had been steadfast in my resolve against continuing our relationship, if you could even call it that. Bill could have asked any number of women to be his date, but he asked me, and there could only be one reason why. He wanted us to work, and sadly that wasn't going to happen. I had selfishly given him hope, just because I wanted more smokin' hot sex.

Then, right on the heels of that insight, I duly dismissed it. I'd been honest with Bill regarding my intentions from day one. It wasn't my fault he kept coming back for more. If he was on a mission to change my mind, that was his exercise in futility.

As I rounded the corner, heading down the path the last quarter mile to my building, I realized how happy I was that he'd called and I picked up my stride.

On Friday, I texted Laura to let her know I wouldn't be able to make happy hour as there was just too much to do before the Montreal trip. I didn't tell her about the looming overnight at Bill's mom's because she would have told me I was full of shit.

When I got home after work, I poured a glass of Crossings Sauvignon Blanc and walked into the closet to consider what I would wear to the party. My eyes roamed left and right across the pink, orange, and turquoise selections, but settled on a navy number I had purchased online a few months prior. It was a very fitted cotton and Lycra dress, with a low square neckline and a wide pink stripe down the middle front and back. It was marketed as a dress that complimented any figure, proof of which was presented via a canvas of countless weather girls from various local news stations sporting the dress in a variety of colors as they romanced the green screen. And although it wasn't quite my style, it was only $29.99. I had hung it in my closet with the tag still on and forgotten about it.

I was about to try the dress on over my Spanx but that would have been redundant compression, so I squeezed out of the onesie and reached into my underwear drawer for a bra I wore back in the day when I could still get a rise out of Lance. I put it on and adjusted it accordingly, thinking "this is way too young for me"—words I'd heard my 84-year old mother utter many times, although not because she was arranging her rangoons in a fuchsia push-up with nipple cutouts. I pulled on the matching crotchless panties—this was no time for half measures. I worked the dress into place and slipped into the pink platform stiletto pumps, another impulse buy. I wobbled as I walked across the plush bedroom carpet to the full-length mirror.

At first glance, I was disappointed in the ensemble, but I had to admit, my dubious selections were figure flattering, and considering my ulterior motive for saying yes to this shindig, the outfit was on point. The what-to-wear decision having been made, I retired to the La-Z-Boy and polished off the bottle of wine watching *From Here to Eternity*. Great story, great acting, and my kind of ending.

CHAPTER NINE

Play in Two Parts

I awoke as I did most mornings, without alarm, but rather slowly, naturally, warmly, as the sun broke through the shell of the horizon, penetrating the bedroom blinds and painting the cream colored walls with parallel lines of red and gold. I had really splurged on this little beach fixer, and it still needed some fixing, but the daily seascape reveal had been worth the weighty mortgage.

My Montreal checklist was on the bedside table. I reached for my glasses and considered it before rising and preparing for my departure. I sped through the next four hours of house cleaning, packing, and laundry, dodging the urge to dwell on the impending rendezvous with Bill until there was nothing more to do but dwell. So, I stepped out the back door and made my way to the water's edge: low tide affording me a flat, firm, right-of-way. As I ambled south along the foamy fringe, my free form disorganized ideas of what would transpire at the Finally Fall party began to coalesce around a central theme: get in, get busy, get going. But how to do it without the inevitable scrutiny from Bill's mother and her friends, that was the question. One thing was for sure, Bill would not be spending the night with me in the carriage house. No, we'd have to bow-chick-a-wow-wow during the party. And that's when I began to formulate a plan.

The adventurous lingerie and rack-revealing dress were still on the chair where I had laid them the night before. Committed, I suited up for the assault.

Mirror check.

Second thoughts.

About my outfit.

About my plan.

About my motive.

Why hadn't I told Bill about Montreal before accepting the invitation? There was really no good reason not to. Instead, I had concocted an elaborate and triple-x rated play in two parts that I knew would leave him wanting more. But the operative word in that last sentence is leave, and leave I would, very early the next morning. Sure, he'd be sad but . . .

I beg your pardon. I never promised you a rose garden.

During the drive to Sundown Beach, I ran my plan over and over in my mind, visualizing Bill's reaction when I finally got him alone and topped him off with a knee trembler. Eventually, I found myself pulling up to a large metal gate and I realized I was nervous. I rolled down the window but couldn't reach the call button. Typical. I cracked the door, slid over, stretched, and pressed the button with the tip of my fingernail. No one answered—the gate just creaked a response and opened, and it didn't close behind me. Apparently, I was the first guest.

The main house looked like a cover on *Coastal Living* magazine. It was a very large Key West style two-story with steps leading up to a deep wrap-around porch, over which teaming planters of purple and yellow flowers hung from the ceiling above the rails. The pale periwinkle structure was trimmed in white and accented by a double yellow door guarded by two unpedigreed cats in rocking chairs. They studied me as I drove slowly past.

Bill bounced into view in his pale blue seersucker shirt and white chinos. Only in Florida can one get away with wearing white pants in the fall and winter.

Regardless, his casual composition was the first indication it would be me that was out of fashion step. He skipped towards me as I stopped the car.

"You made it," he said happily through my window. He pointed to a small cream-colored structure in the distance, close to a bunch of sea grapes that ran parallel to the ocean. "That's the carriage house. Just pull up and park anywhere next to it."

When I reached the carriage house, I parked and grabbed my stilettos from the passenger seat and slipped them on just as Bill reached the car door. He opened it, and I stepped out and up.

"Wow, you grew!" he said.

"Yes, and in the right direction this time, taller instead of wider. Do you like the shoes?" I asked, playfully kicking my leg up behind me.

"I like the whole package," he said, his eyes at half-mast resting on my deep décolletage.

He closed in, preparing for a romantic kiss, and I put my palm on his chest and pressed ever so slightly to stop him.

"Bill, I'm not comfortable with public displays of affection."

"Sure, no problem," he said dryly, backing off. Then under his breath, "Although we aren't really in public."

I could tell he thought I was already putting a damper on the evening but he was able to tamp down any disappointment and manage a smile.

"Where's your bag?" he asked.

I pointed to the back seat, and he opened the door and grabbed my small leather satchel.

"Follow me."

The carriage house was a smaller version of the big house: same Key West style with stairs leading to a wraparound porch. I attempted to navigate the three steps in my stilettos, teetering a little, reinforcing the notion I had worn exactly the wrong thing. I was dressed for a nightclub in Miami. A sundress would have been so much more appropriate. What was I thinking? Oh yeah . . . I was thinking about the old slap-and-tickle.

Bill opened the door and I stepped past him. Shades of white and off-white on bleached wood floors created a seamless flow between the various functional areas in the single open space. The small sofa and loveseat were slip-covered in white cotton duck fabric and placed around an old farm table that had been cut down to coffee table height. The dining table, mismatched chairs, and an antique buffet had been painted off-white and then distressed, making them appear to be part of a coherent set. The bedroom area was delineated by a tan shag rug. White muslin curtains at the end of the bed hung from a rope that ran from one side of the room to the other. The white galley kitchen was a complete setup, but the sink, stove, and fridge were diminutive and to scale.

I could live here, I thought.

I turned to face Bill, but before I could say I love it, he cupped my face in his hands and kissed me softly, briefly on the mouth.

"I didn't think you would come."

I reached for his hands and brought them down, squeezing them a little.

"I'm glad you asked. I've planned something special."

He wrapped his arms around my lower back, still holding my hands, pinning me to him. He murmured, "Tell me," in my ear, his voice dropping an octave, my knees buckling under the weight of it.

"Tell you? No. I'll show you," I said mysteriously. "Can you pour us a glass of wine while I freshen up?"

Bill smiled. "I can do whatever you want."

He picked up my satchel and put it on a luggage rack next to the bed, then headed to the kitchen. I grabbed my ditty bag and went into the bathroom.

I looked in the oval mirror and instinctively reached for my makeup, then stopped myself. This was as good as it got.

Show time.

I walked out and joined Bill at the island counter, on which sat two large glasses of white wine and an ice bucket with the rest of the bottle in it. He stood up off the stool as I approached and handed me a glass of Geyser Peak Sauvignon Blanc. We tapped glasses and took a sip, puzzlement overlaying Bill's chipper countenance.

"This is the wrong outfit for your mom's party, Bill," I said, confusing him further, "but I'll bet ten years from now you'll still be able to recall every stitch. I'd like to model it for you—demonstrate its salient features, but you have to promise me you'll stay right where you are. Can you do that?"

Bill nodded, his amused expression daring me to live up to my bold pronouncement. He rested his arm on the counter and made himself more comfortable.

I picked up my wine and strode to the coffee table, then took one last sip before setting the glass down.

"The thing about the dress," I said, gripping the flexible neckline and working it slowly over my shoulders, exposing the straps of the delicate fuchsia lace, "is that it provides very easy access to the bounty beneath it."

Bill shifted uncomfortably in his seat. I stopped the striptease and looked at him with counterfeit curiosity.

"Do you think I'm too old for sexy lingerie, Bill?"

"No . . . no . . . definitely not, Sally, and when the time comes," he said, glancing nervously at the front door and wide open windows, "I'll be happy to help you off with it."

"Why bother taking it off?" I said, emboldened by his uneasiness, then I jerked the low square neckline of the dress down and up under my pink peekaboo push-up bra. Bill's eyes laser-locked on the exposed gun barrels of my heavy artillery and stiff alarm spread across his neck and shoulders. I smoothed the dress back into place.

I bent over the coffee table in an exaggerated attempt to retrieve my wine glass, my straight legs elongated by the 4-inch heels. I leaned forward and pressed my left palm into the table, careful not to careen into it, then ran my right hand up my leg, taking the hem of the dress up over my hip. I glanced over my right shoulder at Bill. He was quiet, serious, spellbound, his focused surveillance wrapping me like a warm blanket on a cold night.

"These are the matching panties," I said, matter-a-fact. "I've been waiting for a reason to wear them again."

I spun and sat down on the coffee table, my knees high, the hem of the dress forced to my upper thighs, revealing just enough to cause Bill to grip the edge of the stool with both hands and fight with himself to remain seated.

"They're crotchless," I said, smiling at him.

I put my middle finger into my mouth and then dragged it out slowly before sliding my hand up the inside of my thigh to my center.

A bead of sweat trickled down Bill's temple. He wiped it with his bulging bicep.

Then outside . . . a shadow.

I could barely react before the door was flung open. I grabbed the wine in my left hand, stood up, and brought the glass to my lips.

"Geez, I'm sorry," said the interloper, placing a towering vase of beautifully arranged fresh cut flowers on the dining table. He was a younger version of Bill but with some hair. I caught Bill's eye; he was furious.

"I didn't mean to barge in. Mom asked me to get these flowers on the table yesterday, but it slipped my mind."

He reached for my right hand.

"You must be Sally," he said. "I'm Johnny."

And then instead of shaking it, Johnny raised my hand to his lips and kissed it. He looked up at me and kissed it again, this time more openly, breathing in deeply through his nose. After an uncomfortably long pause, he finally let go of me, tearing his eyes from mine to glance at Bill, who was now standing, his arms crossed with impatience.

"Geyser Peak Sauv Blanc," Johnny said, striding behind the counter and reaching for a wine glass, but Bill was heading for the door.

"Tell Mom we'll be there soon," Bill said curtly, holding the door open.

Johnny put the empty glass down.

"All right bro, see you there. And Sally," he pointed at me as he walked past, "can't wait to get to know you better." He winked and he was gone.

I said "Holy shit" and Bill said "I'm going to kill him" at the same time.

"Bill, I think he might have watched a little before he came in. He sniffed my hand like a dog." I couldn't help but giggle, but Bill didn't see the humor in it.

"I've never seen him kiss a woman's hand in my life!" Bill said angrily. "He's got a big mouth. He'll go back and tell my brother Doug and then the news will spread like wildfire!"

"Honestly, as long as your mother doesn't find out, I don't care." I didn't reveal that I hoped the brothers would be jealous of Bill's good fortune. It turned me on.

"But you just told me you don't like public displays of affection!"

"Well, we aren't really in public, are we," I said, throwing Bill's own sentiments back at him. He began pacing between me and the front door.

"I just don't want you to be embarrassed," he said.

"Well, if they say anything, can't you just smile like you're having a great time? I mean, aren't you?" I asked, fishing for reassurance that my provocative production shouldn't be canceled mid-performance.

Bill took a deep breath and walked towards me, putting his hands on my shoulders and exhaling his response in my ear.

"Sally, that was so . . . so unexpected . . . If I would have known, I would have closed the blinds and locked the door. I guess I'm just really disappointed we were interrupted."

I stepped back and looked up at him, grinning mischievously.

"It's OK, that part was over anyway. Well, almost. I was going to put my finger in your mouth, but your brother got to it first."

"I'm going to kill him," he said, then chuckled.

I put my arms around Bill's neck.

"Tonight during the party, I want to meet you somewhere in the house—a bathroom, a closet, the attic—someplace crazy where I can get my mouth on you."

I moved my hand down to Bill's waistband and tugged on it.

"Me and this outfit, Bill? We're going to rock your world tonight."

"Jesus," he whispered, just before his lips touched mine. And I realized that was the first time I had ever heard him swear.

CHAPTER TEN

Two-Story or Ranch?

Bill's cell rang with an old-fashioned rotary ringtone. I found it irritating. He knew who it was before pulling the cell from his pocket.

"I need to take this," he said apologetically, walking away. Then to the phone, "Hi Mom."

He sat on the edge of the kitchen stool and continued the conversation. I picked up my wine and walked to the front window and looked out while still listening in. I couldn't hear what she was saying, but Bill said: "Sally is here. I'm getting her settled in."

And, "Well, where are the boys?"

And, "Johnny was just here."

And finally, "OK, no problem. I'll be right there."

He put his phone back in his pocket.

"I'm sorry, Sally. I've got to go help Mom. She doesn't know where my brothers are. I didn't tell her they were probably on the beach smoking pot."

He laughed, but I couldn't tell if he was joking or not.

"Mind if I take a quick look in the mirror?"

"What for?" I said. "You look positively edible."

He didn't recognize that as the foreshadowing that it was. He just glanced down with an aw shucks grin then walked into the bathroom. Seconds later he came back out and headed for the front door.

"Just text me when you're ready and I'll come get you," he said as he rushed past.

"Not necessary. I would like to make a solo appearance," I said with dramatic flair.

"All right, then. Come out on the porch and I'll show you where to make your grand entrance."

He opened the door and we stepped outside.

"Don't bother going around to the front," he said, his warm hand on my back. "That side door there," he pointed, "leads to the kitchen. The other option is the path along the line of sea grapes from here to the back patio." Bill swept his arm south to north as if presenting the ocean view. "That's typically where all the guests gather, OK honey?"

I winced a little at his term of endearment and hoped he hadn't noticed.

"OK. I'm going to freshen up and have another glass of wine. And Bill?" He was on his way down the porch steps but stopped and looked back up at me. "Don't forget."

It was apparent by the look on his face that he had indeed forgotten, but then a light went on.

"That's the last thing I'd forget," he said with a wink. "I'll be texting you from an undisclosed location as soon as the party gets underway."

I smiled back and gave a little wave, and he tore off across the wide driveway towards the kitchen door.

I looked at my watch; one hour to kill. I walked into the bathroom and considered the spa-like menagerie of high-end toiletries resting on a basket of fluffy white towels on a tiled table. I turned on the tap and poured a generous amount of lavender oil into the claw foot tub, then I undressed and sat down in the two inches of tepid water and leaned back and relaxed while the tub continued to fill. I laid there for a good 45 minutes, draining the cooling water and refilling the tub with hot, thinking about Bill and my plan to shock-and-awe him. Then

I imagined the look on his face when I delivered the big au revoir.

Poor Bill. Undoubtedly, he'd feel a little victimized by the experience when he woke to find me gone. But as far as victimhood went, I was the poster girl, and I was due. I would not let myself be swept into someone else's dream when I had unfulfilled dreams of my own. For once I was going to do what was in my best self-interest, and if I wanted to sleep with other people then I would. Not just because it felt good. Not just for the story. But because it was MY DAMN TURN!

Holding the railing tightly, I descended the stairs in my stilettos and surveyed the route between the carriage house and the kitchen. The ground was a mix of stamped concrete and crushed stone, a high heel nightmare. The path along the sea grapes that led to the back of the house, however, was paved and flat, so I headed down it towards the music.

When I reached the patio, I saw a long line of party-goers under a large white tent making small talk while they waited impatiently at a makeshift bar. Two young bartenders dressed in white shirts and black pants were working feverishly to satisfy the demand. Luckily, a waitress appeared with a tray of champagne. I picked up a glass and thanked her.

Three sips into it, I noticed Bill dragging a large cooler on wheels from the back of the house to the bar. He set it down then pulled out a bottle of Corona, opened it, and took a long draw. I watched him as he interacted with a few of the guests, smiling and shaking hands. His very high likability quotient, combined with that smile, had a magnetizing effect on me so I wasn't surprised when a group of five women, all finely appointed in their size-2 sundresses, approached him. They circled like a committee of starving vultures daring each other to take the first bite, each in turn expertly pulling his handshake close to their body, prompting him to bend down and kiss their cheek so they could whisper something in his ear. I thought about interrupting the feeding frenzy, but before I could, he happened to glance in my direction, then excused himself and hustled over.

"Working hard?" I asked with a smirk.

"Yeah, I haven't stopped moving since I got here. I'm ready to relax and enjoy myself." He smiled and gently clinked his beer bottle against my fragile glass. "I'd like to introduce you to my family, if that's OK. They've been asking for you."

"Sure," I said, thinking I might as well get it over with before I drank too much.

Bill gestured towards the open sliders that led inside the house, and I walked into a large area where a few people were milling around and socializing. The focal point of the space was a stunning portrait of Bill's family sitting on a beach blanket on the sand, the ocean waves crashing in the background. It was hung above a very large brick fireplace painted white to match the walls. I recognized Senator Pruitt. I wanted to stop and study it more closely, but Bill was steering me in the opposite direction.

"They'll be in the kitchen," he said.

The kitchen was homey and cozy despite being so large. Four women were bustling around the big island, preparing this and that for the guests. I pushed Bill back and shook my head.

"Now is not a good time, they're obviously very busy."

"Trust me, now is definitely the time," he said. "They've been wondering why you didn't come over with me an hour ago."

He gently nudged me forward.

"EVERYONE!" he bellowed, garnering their full attention. "THIS IS SALLY."

It rang out like an official and jubilant proclamation at a grand celebration.

"Hello," I said, much subdued in comparison. "Sorry to interrupt."

The woman I guessed was Bill's mom wiped her hands on her apron and approached me, smiling. I extended my hand to meet hers.

"You must be Mrs. Pruitt."

"Call me June," she said, shaking it. "I'm so happy you could join us."

She was slight in build and meticulously coiffed, with blue-gray hair done in an updo. She looked relatively hearty for a woman in her early eighties, but still not nearly as spry and youthful as my own mother, who was a few years older.

"We're in the thick of it right now, dear, but I do look forward to sitting down with you at some point during your visit."

She could tell I was about to offer my help, and I was glad when she stopped me.

"Now you and Bill go and spend some time together. You have no idea how happy he is that you're here."

Well, I certainly knew how happy he was ABOUT to be. She smiled again, then went back to her party prepping.

"Can't believe Billy finally got a date," said a tall thin woman as she walked out of the kitchen with a king-kong sized tray of shrimp cocktail. "I'm Lisa, by the way," she said over her shoulder as she passed, her long dark braid swinging behind her like a heavy rope.

"That's Johnny's ex-wife," Bill said. "She's a real character."

I thought it was nice Lisa could participate in these family gatherings despite the divorce. Lance's dad was still alive, but failing, and I hadn't seen him in a long time. Maybe it was time I did.

"Hi Sally, I'm Rosie, and this is Dougy's wife, Deb."

Bill's sister was a short, slight redhead with pale skin. She favored her mother, and neither possessed the same strong wide facial features and frame as Bill and Johnny. She was brushing egg on little square bundles of puff pastry. Doug's wife, Deb, a rustic looking young woman, obviously from hearty stock, was delicately depositing deviled eggs onto the dimpled dishes designed specifically to hold them. My stomach growled.

The side door swung open and Bill caught it and held it there. Johnny and a man who looked like his twin walked through it, each carrying a case of what I suspected was wine.

"And here comes trouble," Bill said, shutting the door behind them.

"There she is!" said Johnny as he walked past me on his way to the patio. He gave me a knowing nod and winked, as if we shared a secret. I winked back. The twin put his case of wine on the counter and extended his arm.

"We haven't met," he said, gently squeezing my hand. "I'm Doug."

And then just like Johnny, Doug raised my hand to his lips and kissed it slowly, glancing up at me. In turn I glanced at Bill. His arms were crossed in annoyance. He was so easy to read.

Doug continued, "It's nice to see Bill was able to find a real date. He usually brings his imaginary friend, Brancy, to these soirées."

Everyone laughed except June, who shook her head at me as if to suggest she had her hands full raising this family. I let Bill lead me back through the increasingly crowded living area and onto the patio, turning to snag another glass of champagne from the server as she walked behind me.

"Thanks, Sally," Bill said appreciatively, rubbing my arm. He looked like he wanted to kiss me, and this time I didn't resist quite as much. I leaned into him just a little and turned my head, and he discreetly brushed my cheek with his lips and then whispered in my ear, "Ten minutes."

I returned to the living room, tingling with the voltage Bill had just delivered with his tender kiss and message. I moved to the fireplace to get a better look at the portrait and, on closer inspection, realized it was a black and white photo that had been painted. I guessed Bill must have been around 18 when it was taken.

"Do you like it?" said a spindly man in a dark suit who had magically appeared on my right. He was holding a large martini, and a bird sitting on the edge of the glass was helping him drink it. The bird was gray with a yellow head and a rich red dot on its cheek.

"Is that a cockatiel?" I asked, surprised.

"Very good," the man replied. "I'm Andrew Parsons, and this is Harvey Parsons."

I laughed.

"Hello Harvey."

"Hello," Harvey squawked.

"My son painted this old photograph of the Pruitts a few years ago. I think it's very impressive, if I do say so myself," said Mr. Parsons.

"Very impressive. Very impressive," Harvey said, mimicking his owner.

"Yes, it's lovely," I said, then added, "Sally Shaw."

I extended my hand and Mr. Parsons shook it.

"You're here with Bill," he said gently, his eyes

twinkling tipsy. "Such a fine fellow—really had a run of bad luck."

"Bad luck?" I asked coyly, attempting to charm a dossier of details from him.

"Well, you must know his wife died. Dana, lovely girl." he said. "And then the business with that other woman."

"Yes. Jane something or other, I think her name is," I said.

"The way he was treated at that place . . . so embarrassing," Mr. Parsons said, pursing his lips and shaking his head. "He should have resigned in protest."

I was more than intrigued but just then my phone vibrated.

"Excuse me, I'm sorry," I said.

Mr. Parsons hiccuped, and Harvey aped a bird version of it. Then the man nodded and returned to admiring his son's handiwork.

I looked down at my cell to read the text.

Bill: From front foyer, upstairs, third door on right

Excitedly, I made my way through the crowd, smiling and nodding, moving with a purpose so I wouldn't get stopped for conversation, then past Bill's mom who was sitting with her older guests.

I almost made it.

"There she is now. Sally!"

I turned around. Bill's mother was waving me over.

"Sally, I want you to meet my dearest friends."

Having no other option, I smiled and approached them.

"This is Joe Sinatra from Miami Beach; of course, we all call him Frank." They laughed, and I guessed this was the joke that kept on giving. I joined in with the hilarity. "And this is his wife, Annette," June added.

I shook their hands. They looked like you would expect a well-to-do couple in their eighties from Miami Beach would look: slim, tan, well-dressed.

Next were neighbors, Martha and Reece, who looked more like brother and sister, like Humpty and Dumpty. And then finally, best friend Louise. She was elephantine in size and color and gave off an I'm depressed and for a good goddamn reason vibe. I took an instant dislike to her.

"Sally is Bill's new girlfriend," June said, proudly.

Before I could think better of it, I shook my head and said, "Not girlfriend."

June's face fell. Frank and Annette raised their eyebrows. Martha looked confused. Reece excused himself to get a refresher. Louise snickered.

"I'm sorry, dear. Did I misspeak?" June asked, looking as if she had just committed a very serious faux pas.

"No, no," I said. "You just caught me off guard. At 55, I haven't been called anyone's girlfriend in a very long time."

"Well, you certainly don't look 55, Sally, not in that get-up," Louise said, coolly.

Ouch.

"Where is Bill?" June asked.

"I was just going to look for him," I responded, taking advantage of the question. "Very nice meeting you all."

As I skittered away from them and towards the front door, I felt my cell vibrate again. No point answering it; I knew who it was.

Luckily, no one was in the foyer. I traveled quickly up the stairs and counted the doors on the right. The second door was open; it was a bathroom. I tapped lightly on door number three and it opened a crack. Then it opened wider, and Bill grabbed my hand and pulled me in, wrapping me in his arms.

"Thank God," he whispered, "I thought you changed your mind."

"Hell no," I said with a laugh. "I got caught in your mom's web of friends. They're all very nice, except that Louise."

Bill raised his finger to his lips in a shhhh gesture as he locked the door, and then pointed to another door on my right.

"That's a bathroom. Someone might be in there while we're in here."

I nodded a 10-4.

Bill relaxed his grip and I looked around the room. The white plantation shutters were closed and the light was low, just a flicker from two candles Bill had lit to set the mood, but my eyes were adjusting. It was a bedroom outfitted in the finest Tommy Bahama furnishings: a four-poster bed with pineapple carvings on the posts, flanked by two matching bedside tables on which a stack of wood-carved baby sea turtles provided the base for the unlit lamps. An imposing chest of drawers topped with an equally impressive mirror took up most of the deep sage wall to my left. The California King bed, covered in a muted tropical bedspread, was buttressed at the end by a low-back brown leather loveseat. The room was masculine in style and immaculate in presentation.

"Whose room is this?" I asked, already knowing the answer, even though there was nothing personal in the room to indicate it.

"Mine."

"Is it always this neat?"

"It is when Mom's having a party. Don't look in the closet though."

He smiled and reached for my hand, and for a moment he looked like a timid teenager hoping to get his banana peeled for the first time while his parents were out of town. I moved closer, gazed up at him, and slowly ran my right hand down his chest past his stomach, then gently pressed the heel of my hand against his zipper, reaching lower with my fingertips.

Startled, he drew in a breath and snapped his legs together. He put his hands on my shoulders and pulled me in for a romantic kiss, but I turned my head away. Kissing wasn't part of the very well-choreographed performance I had so meticulously planned during my beach walk. Instead, I began unbuttoning and unzipping his pants. I tried to pull them down, along with his boxers, but he was fighting me, trying to pull them back up. I yanked them down with one hand and thrust him backwards onto the loveseat with the other.

"That bathroom door is locked, right?" I asked, angling my head towards it.

Bill squeaked, "Yes," like a scared kitten.

I dropped to my knees and wedged myself between his legs. His six shooter was as limp as a cooked spaghetti noodle. If I could have flung it across the room and hit the wall, it would have stuck.

I breathed along his length, closer and closer, until the tip of my tongue lightly grazed it. He startled again, but I continued the kinetics, advancing with more and more contact until I was gliding along him from stem to stern, drawing him into my mouth and nursing him hard for a few seconds, then releasing with a popping sound that made him jump, as if a firecracker had gone off under his feet.

"Do you like this?" I asked, knowing that under normal circumstances this was just about the stupidest question anyone could ask a man. But here in his childhood bedroom, in his mother's house, with an increasing number of guests congregating below us, the circumstances were anything but normal.

"Yes," Bill answered hoarsely. And then clearing his throat, "It feels great."

He grew with my persistence, his anxious expression belayed by his budding bagpipe. He watched zombie-like as I dribbled a four-inch stream of saliva onto the head of his hammer, then he moaned an "Oh my God" as I went to work on him, stroking, licking, nipping, flicking. At that moment, I had complete power over Bill. I could have told him to buy me a house and he would have responded, "Two-story or ranch?"

I stood abruptly and Bill lurched backwards in angst, his hands slapping wide against the cool leather seat, his legs firing out straight and landing akimbo. I gently kissed the top of his smooth head, then put him on notice.

"Better relax, Bill. I'm just getting started."

I turned my back to him, then moved my legs to the outside of his, dragging the dress up over my hips, exposing the fuchsia lace crotchless panties that I knew he wasn't surprised to see—not after the carriage house tease. As I guided him through the opening, I heard him exhale the words, "Oh Jesus."

Bill unwound and began taking initiative as I rode him reverse cowgirl, the electric caress of his left hand gliding up the inside of my bare thigh, his other hand climbing my back beneath the flexible fabric of the dress, finding the bra's double hook-and-eye closure, and in one swift sweep of his nimble fingers, it was open.

I reclined against him and reached overhead for the back of the couch, and he nipped at my neck, his hand moving around to my breast, kneading it and rolling the nipple between his fingers, his other hand inching under the lace panties, finding my fancy bit and coaxing it to a stony bloom. Quiver.

We rocked in erotic tempo and I closed my eyes and let him take me to the brink of deliverance. But just.

I stood and turned to face him, his anxiety gone, the fever of desire reddening him. He grabbed my leg and my arm and pulled me to him, desperate to reunite. I stared into his aqua eyes as I inched myself down onto him.

"You fill me so perfectly," I said longingly. It had a ring of commitment to it, which was unintentional, but Bill heard what he wanted to hear.

"We're a perfect fit, Sally," he responded, pulling me by the back of my neck to him for what we knew would be the last kiss before the wham. It was soft and familiar at first, then increasingly open and wet, then frantic with anticipation.

I fell forward against his heaving chest, bracing my left arm against the back of the loveseat, pressing my glistening cleavage against his chin. Escorted by his hot breath, the swirl of his tongue skated under the neckline of my dress. When he discovered my puckered nipple and sucked it forcefully into his mouth, thunder rumbled deep into me, and the lightning that followed struck its target.

CRACK!

The starting pistol went off in my head and with it the dash to climax. I ground against him with determined fury, leaving him to manage his own pleasure.

"Oh yeah, oh yeah, OH YEAH!" I chanted to the rhythm of my rocking, lost in my own objective, but still vaguely aware of Bill's warm hand melting down my backside and sneaking beneath the lacy elastic. When he found my starfruit and gently circled its circumference, I arched and gasped.

Taking that as a yes, Bill pulsed the soft pad of his middle finger against the backdoor, testing the lock, while he bucked up against me like an untamed bronco. I was aware of the frenzied moans and groans of my own voice—louder they came like a freight train barreling towards me, prompting Bill to put his hand over my mouth in an attempt to stifle the sound. When the tip of his finger penetrated the resistive portal, I short-circuited.

I collapsed on him, covered in the sweat of total fuck-euphoria, but he was still moving beneath me, cooing in my ear, and I realized I had left him behind. I lifted off of him and crumpled to my knees, weak but determined to complete my mission. He ran his fingertips along my scalp, and I could feel his heart beat banging through them. When I once again took his scarlet shape shifter into my mouth, he knotted my damp curls in his hands and groaned with gratification.

Almost immediately, the corner of my eye caught the green digital display on Bill's clock radio and I alarmed. Becoming more determined in my methods, I intensified my grip on him and accelerated the action, my lips moving in meter with my stroke, my left hand cupping his boys and jostling them gently between my fingers. Bill's hands were white-knuckling the rolled ends of the loveseat, his gaze meeting my own, his crystal blue eyes narrowing, darkening, his face contorted in delirium as the storm brewing deep in his loins threatened to overtake him. I could taste the approaching tsunami.

"It's been so long . . . so long . . . since it was this good," he moaned, and his hips slid forward and his head fell back.

When I worked my fingers behind his berries, pressing up into that special stretch of skin, stimulating his prostate, he lost it.

"Oh . . . GOD . . . SALLY . . . I'm going to . . . to . . . TO!!!"

It was my best effort, inducing the agonizing ecstasy I intended, as well as a welcome relief that I could still command it. I didn't shush his uncontrolled enthusiasm, but if there was someone in that bathroom, they were getting an earful.

I loosened my grip on him and he faded back into the loveseat, his head swinging slowly from side to side until it decelerated to stillness. He was mumbling some gibberish, but I thought I heard the words "heart attack." I squeezed his wrist, thankfully finding a pulse.

"Bill," I said, shaking him a little, "we've got to get back to the party."

I knocked once on the bathroom door and waited. No one answered, so I went in and locked the door facing the hall. I ran the tap.

"Bill!" I whispered loudly at him again, "Get UP! We have to go back!"

He appeared disoriented, as if he had awoken from a long dream. He was standing now, stumbling, trying to do up his pants.

"How long have we been here?"

"A long time!" I whisper-yelled, unable to do the math. I cleaned myself up, smoothed my clothing, and took measure of myself in the mirror. I had that glowy, dreamy-eyed, tousled, just bonked look— pretty attractive, really, but if we returned to the party together, it would be patently obvious that Bill had been giving me more than just a tour of the house. When I returned to the bedroom to instruct him to give me a five-minute head start, I found him on the bed, his hands folded neatly on his stomach, his feet crossed at the ankles, a gentle snore rumbling in his throat.

CHAPTER ELEVEN

Big Breakup Scene

I peeked over the railing; luckily, the foyer was empty. I began navigating the steps gingerly in my stilettos, gripping the wooden stair rail with both hands. It was a lot more difficult going down than it had been coming up. I was almost at the bottom when June appeared, placing her mottled hand on the knobbed end of the banister.

"Oh, Sally, do you know where Bill is?" She looked concerned.

"I was wondering the same thing," I said, like the good little liar I am. "I hope it's OK I was upstairs. The downstairs bathrooms were occupied."

"Of course, it's fine, dear. I just don't understand what's gotten into Bill. This is the second time today he has been late or a no-show." She sounded frustrated. "His brothers need help with the tiki bar."

June raised her chin as her eyes arched up the two-story staircase, as if she was considering the climb to find her wayward eldest.

"You know, I just realized I am starving!" I said, distracting her. "Is the food down at the tiki bar?"

"Heavens no, all the food is out on the patio," she said, taking my arm and leading me back into the living room, pointing beyond the glass sliders. "Didn't you see that big white tent? There's a buffet out there with cracked lobster and stone crab claws, ceviche, spring rolls, curry coconut shrimp . . ."

I was salivating.

"Sounds wonderful, June, thanks. And I'll text Bill right now and let him know you're looking for him."

"Thank you, dear, and I apologize for his behavior. You are his guest; he should be more attentive." She patted my hand. "He certainly has been a bad boy today," she said, as she headed for the kitchen.

Oh, you have no idea.

Once on the patio, I loaded a plate, then couldn't find a place to sit. I walked down the wooden bridge towards the ocean and came upon the aforementioned tiki bar, complete with outdoor kitchen basics and the essential thatched roof. Doug and Johnny were passing out cold beer and wine to some of the party-goers who had decided to enjoy a bonfire on the beach. The evening breeze was delightful and had whipped up the flames, revealing the happy faces.

"Hi Sally," Johnny said, pleased to see me. "What can I get ya?"

"Sauvignon Blanc?" I asked, and he quickly poured me a glass of the same Geyser Peak that Bill had put in the carriage house.

"Mind if I sit here and eat?"

"Please, sit down," Doug said. "Where's Bill?"

"No idea," I said, biting into a mini beef wellington. Yummy. The brothers looked at me with skepticism. My cell vibrated loudly.

"That's probably him now," I said as I pulled it from my purse. It was a text, but it wasn't from Bill. I didn't recognize the number, but the area code was 514, and I knew that was Montreal. Was it Jeff? Or was it the man I had zipless designs on, Marco Lamont?

Marco was a contractor associated with SEA, so hooking up with him was probably not the best idea, and been-there-done-that. But he was many miles away from Sydney, and at 37, it was doubtful he would consider me a possible life partner. As far as our relationship went, we were just friendly coworkers. Still, he was a flirt, and whenever our paths would cross, he made it clear he was willing. I was married then and had no intention of doing anything untoward. Now that had changed, and I was looking forward to suggesting otherwise.

514: It's Marco Lamont. Heard you would be here Monday

Me: Yeah coming up for a month or so

514: Fantastic. Thursday happy hour at Flanagans

Then Lisa showed up.

"Where the hell is Bill?" she said to Johnny, hands on hips. "Your mother is pissed."

514: Dinner and party the following Saturday. I hear you have no excuse now ;)

Me: OK see you soon

514: Can't wait cherie

Before I put the phone away, I texted a Where are you? message to Bill.

Another 15 minutes and another Sauvignon Blanc.

"Something's wrong," Johnny said abruptly. "I'm going to look for him."

Oh God, I prayed, please let Bill show up. And miraculously, he did.

"Well look what the cat dragged in," said Lisa. "Where the hell have you been?"

Bill approached me at the bar, grinning, and put his arm around me.

"Calm down, Lisa. I took a bit of a dizzy spell so I had a little lay-down in my room. Feelin' great now though."

Lisa looked at her brothers with a quizzical expression and mouthed the two words "dizzy spell" as if she'd never heard them put together before. Doug shrugged, Johnny looked suspicious. Bill missed his sibling's silent communications and kissed me on the mouth. I didn't object, I guess because I felt so damn good about everything: the hot beef injection in Bill's boyhood bedroom, the promising promotional opportunity in Montreal, and the chance to play hide the cannoli with that French Canadian Fabio, Marco Lamont.

Doug opened a bottle of Corona and passed it to Bill, who took it from him and uncharacteristically drained it in three big gulps. We all watched, united in our surprise, and then Doug passed him another. He held onto that one, smiling ear to ear.

"What's that on the top of your head?" Lisa asked, pulling Bill's head forward by the back of it. "Is that lipstick?"

"Ah . . . that's my fault," I said with a giggle, elbowing Bill. Lisa, Johnny, and Doug were watching us with increased interest, possibly cluing in to our little secret.

"You have a very bewitching smile, Sally," Doug said admiringly.

"Thanks" I said. "Bill was just saying I have the whitest teeth he's ever come across, weren't you, Bill?"

Bill looked at me, eyes wide. Lisa arched her brows. I popped the last bit of food in my mouth and held my empty glass towards Doug, prompting him to refill it. Bill stood up.

"I'm starving," he said, turning to me.

"Well, allow me to fix you a plate." I stood to join him. "Thanks," I yelled over my shoulder as we walked across the wooden bridge towards the patio, arms linked.

"I thought you wanted to keep everything on the down-low, Sally," Bill said, mildly amused.

"Well, I guess I've got a little of the devil in me," I said, looking behind us to make sure the coast was clear. Then I grabbed his ass and he jumped.

"You sit down," I said, pulling out an empty chair for him at a vacant table. "What would you like?"

"It's Mom's cooking, so all of it. Except the guacamole, she puts jalapenos in it."

I made my way to the chow line, piling the food high on the plate. As soon as I put it in front of him, he dove in enthusiastically.

"It's nice to see you eat something besides salad," I said, smiling at him.

Bill fought to swallow and wiped his mouth.

"I'm picky," he said, and I thought that was just one more reason. But despite all of the reasons not to continue seeing Bill, I couldn't deny the one big reason in his favor. I put my hand on his forearm and squeezed, suppressing a smile into a tight-lipped grin while I considered what to say.

"Is there something on your mind, Sally?" He chuckled, dipping a colossal shrimp in cocktail sauce and biting off just a piece of it, because it was too large to consume whole.

"Well, I just want to say . . ."

"Yes?" Bill said, teasing.

"I want to say thank you."

"Thank you?"

"Yes, thank you for . . . that . . . that . . ."

"My pleasure," he said, dipping another shrimp

in the sauce and winking, his welcome interruption rescuing me from the difficulty of defining our burning carnality.

He wiped his mouth with a napkin and relaxed back in the chair, finishing his beer.

"Why didn't you tell me you're a lawyer, Bill?" I asked casually, but it surprised him. He hesitated.

"I'm not currently practicing law."

"That's not really an answer."

"Everyone in my family is a lawyer, even my mom," Bill said, shrugging, "It's no big deal."

After that ambiguous exchange, it was quiet and still between us while we considered each other. Bill exuded peace, contentment, and balance, while I struggled to hide an uneasiness beginning to creep into my consciousness.

"I'm never going to forget tonight, Bill," I said wistfully, raising my glass. He leaned forward and held his empty bottle against it.

"Don't worry. I won't let you."

We sat there conversing for a while longer. Bill started with details of his beach condo. He was having it remodeled, one of the reasons he had been staying at his mother's so often. He asked for my input, but from the sound of it, the design decisions had already been made. We talked a little about the people we knew at the gym, and then eventually the topic turned to SEA. Bill described a situation with one of SEA's subcontractors in Vermont that he was working to resolve, but I was only half listening. Work-talk reminded me of Montreal, and that I had to tell him about it very shortly.

The band was doing a bang-up job paying tribute to the original artists, no matter the genre. The playlist had started with standards from Frank Sinatra, Doris Day, Dean Martin, and the like, but had gradually morphed into more contemporary tunes. When he realized I had stopped talking and gone introspective on him, Bill stood and reached for my hand. For the next half hour or so, we danced together in the crowd, smiling and laughing, accidentally bumping against others, and sometimes trading off partners. Everything was going so well, and then . . .

"Hey brother, can I cut in?"

It was Johnny.

"Get lost," Bill replied, only half-jokingly.

"Seriously bro, Mom's asking for you. I'll stand in for you until you get back."

Bill's demeanor changed when his mother was mentioned.

"Do you mind, honey?" he asked.

I didn't want to get between Bill and his mother, so I nodded and Bill left me with Johnny. He took my hand and put his other on my back, pulling me closer to him. His demeanor had also changed.

"You're not going to break my brother's heart, are you, Sally?" he asked, frowning, his dark blue eyes vibrating left and right as they searched for the answer in my guarded green ones.

"Johnny, I really need to sit down. These shoes are killing me," I said, truthfully.

I tried to pull away, but he tightened his grip.

"So, is that a yes?" he asked, and I answered him plainly, but not 100% honestly.

"Bill and I aren't right for each other for a whole host of reasons. We've known it since our first date a few weeks ago. We've discussed it. I agreed to come here tonight because he felt pressure to bring someone—pressure from you and your family."

"That's a load of horseshit and you know it!" Johnny snapped in my ear, then softened his tone. "You're the first woman he's brought to this house since Dana died. He told Mom you were his girlfriend. You're acting like you don't know how he feels about you when it's blatantly obvious to everyone else."

"He told your mom I was his girlfriend to make her feel better, not because it's true. Anyway, it really doesn't matter." I shrugged him off, ready to get on with it. "I'm going to Montreal tomorrow for a month for work. I might even stay longer. That'll give Bill the opportunity to meet someone that . . . that wants the same things he does."

Johnny stepped back and glared at me.

"Does he know this?"

"Not yet. I'm going to set things straight tonight. Let me handle it."

Just then I felt Bill's soft hand on my neck.

"Get lost, Johnny, and I mean it this time. Mom needed a carafe from the pantry, for God's sake. Why didn't you just get it for her?"

"You're taller," Johnny said defensively. "I would have had to get a step stool." And then to me, with finality, "Goodbye Sally," and he walked away.

Bill took me in his arms and noticed my agitation.

"What's wrong, did he say something to you?"

I shook my head.

"No, nothing, I . . . I . . . my feet are killing me. I want to sit down, and I really need a drink."

Bill led me inside and sat me down on an over-stuffed, flamingo-print couch in a cozy corner.

"Stay here. I'll get you something."

I took off my shoes and rubbed my feet, then rested my head back and closed my eyes in an effort to gather my thoughts and prepare for the jagged ending of the evening's roller coaster ride.

"Are you feeling OK, my dear?"

I could barely understand him. I opened my eyes. It was Mr. Parsons and Harvey. They were both swaying, both drunk.

"Hello. Yes, I'm just tired, and my feet hurt. I'm afraid I wore the wrong thing tonight." I smiled feebly.

"You are a beautiful woman no matter what you wear," said Mr. Parsons, slurring his words and raising the dwindling martini.

"No matter what, no matter what," slurred Harvey in response, wings flapping as he gripped the see-sawing glass tightly with his claws. And then Bill reappeared with a gin and soda, which I grabbed with both hands and inappropriately gulped.

"Enjoying the party, Andrew?" Bill asked.

"Yes, it's splendid," Mr. Parsons replied. "And this Sally Shaw, so charming."

Parsons winked at me as he and Harvey savored the last few drops of the drink.

"She's very special," Bill said, resting his hand on my shoulder and smiling his magnetic smile.

Parsons and Parsons staggered off and Bill sat down beside me, giving my knee a little love rub. I turned to him, preparing to let him down as easy as humanly possible, but I lost my nerve and something different came out.

"You know we can't sleep together, right?" I said, and surprisingly, Bill agreed.

"Yeah, I know. I'll take some ribbing from the boys but I think Mom will appreciate it. She'll consider it a sign of respect."

"Right. So when I say I'm going to turn in, you can offer to walk me to the door, and I'll say no, and you can kiss me on the cheek, and then I'll go back to the carriage house alone."

"Wow, you plan everything," Bill said with a chuckle.

"I'm a planner, and I like things to work out as planned."

"OK chief." Bill gave me a mock salute, still on cloud nine and completely missing my mood shift.

I allowed our conversation to ramble here and there while watching the crowd continue to thin. Soon almost all of the guests were gone, and Bill's brothers and sister had congregated around us, along with Louise. The other ladies were in cleanup mode in the kitchen, but before too long, June joined us, and Johnny brought her a small glass of dry sherry. And then it was too late and I decided Bill would be hearing about Montreal from Montreal.

He was in a jovial mood, his arm around me, giving me the occasional loving look and a hug and squeeze. His siblings were decidedly more somber. I'm sure it was obvious to them Bill knew nothing about my intention to exit the country as well as our relationship. Anxious to begin the end, I grabbed my shoes and stood up.

"Everyone, it's been such a wonderful evening but I'm afraid I'm going to have to turn in." I smiled at Bill's mother with gratitude. "Thanks so much, June, for including me."

"You are most welcome, my dear. I will be turning in shortly myself. We'll see you in the morning for breakfast."

I nodded affirmatively, despite knowing full well that breakfast with the family wasn't going to happen.

"Yes, you need your rest, Sally," Johnny said. "What with that open-ended work assignment in Montreal."

There was an awkward silence and then Bill stood up to face me, confused. He looked at Johnny, then back at me.

"What open-ended work assignment?"

"I was just telling Johnny when we were dancing," I said, swallowing hard. "I'll be going to Montreal to manage the QuebecNet project on site."

I tried to sound upbeat.

Bill's eyebrows knitted.

"When? For how long?"

"Ah . . . tomorrow actually. Could be a month or maybe more, depending."

"Depending on what?" Bill pressed.

I didn't answer. Instead I threw an angry glance Johnny's way. His arms were crossed in front of him and he was gloating like he had just done everyone a big favor. Doug and Rosie, on the other hand, looked uncomfortable. June was peering down into her sherry.

"Oh now that's a fly in the ointment," Louise said, feigning concern.

The tension was palpable, and Bill went off script.

"I'll walk you to the door," he said forcefully, and I felt I couldn't say no.

We walked without speaking or touching, through the living room, out the kitchen door, and across the driveway. I was barefoot, the uneven and sharp surface slowing my stride. He was already on the stairs of the carriage house when I reached my car.

"Bill! Can we do this out here?"

He paused and turned, and then came back down the stairs to meet me.

"You know, they're probably looking out the window at us," he said.

"I don't care," I said. "Going in there would make this more difficult."

"More difficult for who, you? Because I'm the one who has been blindsided and embarrassed."

I dropped my shoes and put both of his hands in mine and brought them to my chest, holding them tightly. He didn't resist.

"Bill, I'm so sorry. I should have told you about Montreal when you invited me here, and I should have declined the invitation, but I was self—"

"You know, up until five minutes ago, this was one of the best days of my life," Bill said, interrupting my apology. "Why did you tell Johnny instead of me?"

"He was needling me on the dancefloor about our relationship," I said. "He can be an ass, but he really does care about you."

"It's just . . . I mean . . . a month or more? Just when we're getting started?"

"Bill, do you remember our first date at Clams? We were both crystal clear about what we were looking for, and we both knew when we left the restaurant that we weren't a match."

"I do remember that date. I also remember how it ended, and the way you respond every time I get you in my arms."

I let go of his hands and squeezed his upper arms hard with frustration.

"Of course I respond that way, Bill! I'm extremely sexually attracted to you. I physically feel electricity when you touch me. Unfortunately, that doesn't negate the multiple reasons why I can't be your wife!"

Bill stepped back from me. I imagined his family and Louise peering through the blinds watching the drama play out, concluding rightly that this was the big breakup scene.

"Is there someone else?" he asked, like he was afraid of the answer.

"No, not now, but there could be, and undoubtedly there WILL be."

"So, what we did upstairs, that wasn't special?"

"I told you it was."

"But not so special that you won't do the same thing with someone else next weekend."

I didn't respond, but thought of Marco.

It was quiet for a few seconds as neither of us had any more to add.

Bill finally spoke, almost inaudibly.

"Well, I guess that's it then," he said with dignified acceptance, but I knew I had broken something.

Unexpectedly, Bill took my hand and raised it to his lips. He barely kissed it, then turned it over and kissed my wrist, breathing in my perfume like he was attempting to create a memory. Warm voltage hummed from his mouth as it traveled through me, spreading up my arm and across my chest, encircling my heart and compressing it until it hurt. I recognized it for what it was. It was love.

Uncharacteristically overcome with emotion, my eyes filled with tears and I pinched them tight to avoid revealing the feelings I was denying. I heard Bill whisper, "Goodbye," and when I opened my eyes, he was walking away from me towards the main house.

CHAPTER TWELVE

Vieux-Montreal

By 4 am, I was at the front door of the carriage house with my bag and purse. I peeked out the window, hoping everything in the main house would still be dark, and it was. Aware that sneaking off without saying goodbye or thank you to June would be the height of rudeness, I searched for pen and paper and finally found them in the bedside table.

Dear June,

So sorry I had to leave on short notice and could not thank you again in person for your much appreciated hospitality. I hope you can forgive me, for everything.

Sincerely,

Sally Shaw

I backed the car up and around and then very slowly drove up to the gate. Cringing as the gate gears squeaked and rattled open, I nudged through, turned right onto the beach highway, and ten minutes later I was over the causeway and driving north on US 1 towards Sydney. Shortly thereafter, I rolled over Sunday's bagged *Hometown* magazine lying in the driveway and pulled into my garage. The garage door shimmied to a close behind me.

Ahhh, sanctuary.

After repacking a little for Montreal, I checked in with Air Transat and called the SEA limo service; everything was set. At 6:55 am, coffee in hand, I walked out the door and headed towards Clarissa's House of Wax.

"Good morning," I said as I walked through the back door of the salon. "Hey, thanks for accommodating my schedule."

Clarissa looked over her shoulder at me, a silent yawn opening slowly below her droopy eyelids. She smiled weakly and then went back to stirring her little pot of wax. I hiked up my skirt and assumed the position on the recliner.

Clarissa dipped a wooden spatula into the hot vat and pulled it out, twirling the thick purple goop around the stick and blowing on it to cool it. Then she painted it on the left side of my bewhiskered mound and up against my leg. It burned.

"That's HOT!"

"Oh," Clarissa said sarcastically, "such a fragile flower." Then tap, tap, tapping on the wax to gauge precisely when to yank up on the edge of it, she did.

RIPPPPPPPP!!!

"Ouch! DAMN IT!!!"

And so the torture continued, down and under, almost as clinical and intimate as a gynecological exam, until the only fur to be found was a modest triangle on the knoll. Clarissa powdered me up and then turned to my feet.

"What color today?" she asked as she wiped away the emerald green toenail polish.

"I'm thinking black," I said, just to get her reaction. "I mean, it IS Montreal."

"Hell no, you're too old to pull that off."

"Don't remind me," I said, plucking my go-to silver polish from my purse.

I slumped back into the chair and closed my eyes as Clarissa began to work her magic on my swollen, calloused feet. Unexpectedly, Bill's handsome face appeared—his brilliant blue eyes lighting up my dark, quiet mind before pixelating into nothingness——a reminder of what I had rejected. I sighed.

"Everything OK?" Clarissa asked, looking up from her paint job.

"I'm thinking of getting some fillers," I said, apropos of nothing. "My mother has it done every so often. It lifts her face and smooths out the lines."

"I thought about it too," Clarissa said. "Last year, after I went on that Paleo diet. I lost 15 pounds and gained 15 years. My entire face collapsed. Ever been mistaken for your mother's younger sister?"

"Oh yeah," I said truthfully, as my mother is almost criminally youthful.

"Anyway," Clarissa continued, "I decided against it. It's very expensive and it doesn't last half as long as they advertise. I'm saving up for a proper face and neck lift."

"My mom's neighbor had that done; cost her 18 grand," I said, "So, imagine how she felt when the guy power washing her house was able to correctly guess her age. He said he could tell by her hands. Her HANDS!"

"That's depressing," said Clarissa, shaking her head, as she slipped my feet into my flip flops, being careful not to disturb the wet paint.

"So, the face and neck lift won't be enough. We'll need a hand job!" I said.

We giggled.

"And speaking of hand jobs," she said, "are you going to see that French guy who always hits on you?"

"Marco? Yeah, seeing him Thursday for happy hour and maybe dinner and a party the following Saturday. I'm nervous just thinking about it. He's almost 20 years younger than I am and in phenomenal shape—a real gym rat."

"Well I'd love to see you and Marco double-date with Lance and what's-her-name. Give Lance a taste of his own medicine."

"Honestly, Clarissa, I don't know why Marco is so eager to play slophockey with me."

"Maybe he's looking for an older woman," she said. "You know . . . a cougar."

"I am not a cougar!" I said. "I've never been attracted to younger men per se. For the most part, I find them intellectually undeveloped. But I need to get back in the game before I'm too afraid to play. And the universe is putting Marco in my path. I don't think it's a coincidence."

"Nonsense. The universe has nothing to do with it. It's just the circumstances that have changed. So, take advantage of it. You can add your experience to that book of horny stories you're writing."

"I would not characterize my book in that way," I said, rolling my eyes as I reached for my purse.

"Are you kidding? I read The Orlando Schtupp. I couldn't keep my hands off myself! Oh and I hope you don't mind, I kept the printout and I've shown it to a few other clients. They want to see more."

"I hope you didn't put my name to it," I said, alarmed, "If anyone at SEA found out I wrote that, I'd have to resign out of sheer embarrassment."

"No worries. I didn't," she said with a grin. Then the grin faded into a cautionary expression and she added, "So . . . is Bill still in the picture?"

"Not really," I said flatly, digging in my purse.

"Because . . . if it's OK . . . I mean . . . if you're done with him . . . I wouldn't mind an introduction."

She wasn't joking so I didn't know how to respond. I didn't want to think about Bill schtupping any other woman at all, let alone my esthetician. I continued the contrived pursuit of Clarissa's payment for another minute then pulled out my checkbook.

"Sorry, it will have to be a check today," I said, then began filling in the blanks. Happily, my no-cash ruse had been enough to distract her.

"I take it you've packed some condoms," she said.

Condoms. Hmmmmm. I couldn't remember ever buying a condom or the last time I used one. I'd let Bill completely off the hook on that note twice!

"Can't be too careful nowadays," she added, "and I'm guessing this Marco character has plenty of experience parking the beef bus in Tuna Town."

"Parking the beef bus in Tuna Town?!" I said with a laugh. "Well, I thought I'd heard 'em all, but I've never heard that one."

"If I were you, I'd take a pack of regular and a pack of Magnums," Clarissa said thoughtfully, as she wiped down the chair and foot tub.

"Magnums?"

"Yeah. Some guys are too big for regular condoms, and they'll refuse to wear them. Don't take a chance; get both sizes. A dozen each should do it."

"Two dozen? Are you insane?!" I said as I handed her the check. "I'm going to Montreal for work, not for 24 rounds of gland-to-gland combat!"

Clarissa chuckled. "Good one."

Despite my disclaimer, I stepped out into the warming morning and, heeding her advice, crossed the street and entered CVS. I'd been in there a thousand times but had no idea where the condoms were, and I wasn't going to ask for directions. Wandering aimlessly, I finally discovered them in the First Aid aisle.

I guess that makes sense.

Happy to see a female at the pharmacy register, I hurried to pay before anyone else got in line. As I turned to leave, I thought I heard her say, "Have a good lay." But no, I must have imagined it.

✦

"Hey stranger," Laura said when she answered my call. "Where are you?"

"I'm in the company limo on my way to the airport, doing a little writing on the way. I just called to say goodbye and I'll miss you."

"I'll miss you too. And speaking of writing, you better bring me back some juicy stories, although I doubt you'll be able to top The Orlando Schtupp. You making Bill give you his pajama top then watching yourselves in the mirror go at it. GEEZ that was hot!"

I glanced at my laptop monitor and smiled to myself, anticipating her reaction when I finally recited the story I was just putting the finishing touches on: Two-Story or Ranch?

After the call, I stretched out on the long seat, resting my head on a pillow, sleepy but too wound up to actually sleep. I pictured my destination and what might lie in store for me besides work.

Ottawa is the capital of Canada, but Montreal, just a two-hour drive east, is considered the cultural capital. Most people there speak French, but on the street, many other languages are heard. SEA's Montreal office is right downtown, not too far from McGill University. In fact, you can see it through the towering walls of glass from our offices on the 25th floor. The area is bustling with great shops and restaurants. On more than one occasion, I had gotten lost in their underground city, the largest in the world. You can actually live and work in Montreal and avoid ever coming out into its unforgiving winters.

But it was Vieux-Montreal I longed to revisit. This time I would finally take a horse-drawn carriage ride around the cobblestone streets and grand buildings to get that taste of European flavor. I would visit the Notre Dame Basilica, its Gothic revival architecture one of the most dramatic in the world. And I couldn't wait for another plate of authentic French poutine.

And then there was Marco Lamont. Incredibly sexy and charming in that European way, Marco was tall and sinewy with biceps as big as his head; no doubt his dress shirts had to be custom made. His straight blond hair was longish, not quite reaching his shoulders, and he wore it tucked behind his ears. And unlike most men in Montreal, and everywhere else it seems, he had no scruff on his face. That suited me fine, as I like nothing better than a clean-shaven cheek next to mine or between my thighs.

The flight was uneventful, and soon I joined the throng of others navigating through customs. I must have a guilty face because I always got the third degree, but today was the exception to the rule, and after queuing up behind a family of five, I was in a cab, and about 20 minutes later, at the Dormir Suites in Vieux-Montreal. I unlocked the door to my room, number 531, and the lanky young bellboy dragged in the two large suitcases behind me.

"Is there anything else I can do for you, madam?"

"Not right now," I said, smiling and passing him a few dollars.

The door shut and I perused the room. It was just like the ones I'd had on previous trips there: a modern suite with a living room and small kitchen in one room, and a king-sized bed with adjoining bathroom in the other—a perfect short-term residence.

Before unpacking, I called room service and ordered a burger and a bottle of cheap red. I opened my laptop, connected to the hotel Wi-Fi, and navigated directly to my email accounts. Mom and my oldest had sent well-wishing notes, and my youngest was requesting some new sweatpants from Roots, her favorite Canadian store. Nothing of any importance on the work side, and nothing from Bill.

My mission to impress Jeff was relatively successful. He didn't jump up and down and clap his hands, but despite my jittery delivery, the presentation's content was well received, the result being a slew of ad hoc meetings designed to flesh out and finalize what I had proposed.

Before I knew it, it was Thirsty Thursday and I was walking to Flanagan's Irish pub on Chestnut Street. I'd been there many times and enjoyed the cave-like atmosphere and the excellent booze offerings, dozens of single malts and lots of great beers on draft. Guinness is my favorite, but that evening I went astray and ordered a Murphy's.

And then I saw him.

He was waving his arms about, standing in a circle with three very young men I'd never seen, possibly new-hires. I couldn't tell if he was explaining the rotation of the moon around the earth or how to change a light bulb, but the youngsters were hanging on his every word. All four were wearing the stereotypical Montreal-man's business attire—trendy, slim-fitting suits, jackets double-vented in the back, flap pockets and notched lapels. Marco's blue-gray jacket with a sharkskin finish flapped at his sides, exposing the shiny navy-blue lining, as he continued his explanation of whatever it was.

And then there was she: Desirée Danner, a decidedly alpha female at Montreal SEA. She wedged herself between Marco and one of the newbies, and Marco immediately stopped his heretofore uninterrupted commentary to face her. He listened intently as she whispered something in his ear, his hand reaching around to her back and rubbing it a little, the young lads visibly uneasy with the familiarity displayed between he and his administrative assistant.

Marco said something to her, and she nodded and smiled. Then he and the boys watched admiringly as she walked away, her backside rolling in a figure 8. She had a great body, but in my opinion, black jeggings are not appropriate attire at an engineering firm. But that's how it is in Montreal, the men typically out-dress the women.

I continued to watch Marco for a little longer as he schooled the new-hires, and then he saw me, excused himself, and walked slowly but deliberately over to me, never losing eye contact, barely smiling, really turning it on, one foot directly in front of the other like a model on the catwalk.

I'm . . . too sexy for my shirt . . . so sexy it hurts.

"Bonjour, SallEEE!" Marco said, putting his hands on my shoulders and kissing both of my cheeks, a la Français. Inappropriate for colleagues, I thought, especially in public, but maybe I was just being too damned Anglo. He hailed the bartender, who knew what he wanted without asking and began to concoct it.

Still in model mode, Marco squeezed his shoulders together and lowered his arms, gravity slipping his jacket from him, revealing a pale lavender button-down dress shirt that appeared to be painted on, exposing the muscular definition beneath. His suit pants, just as tight, had to be under pressure from what was either a massive tube snake or a rolled up hockey sock.

"Like what you see, SallEEE?" Marco asked, grinning, catching me in the act of meat-gazing.

"Yes, very much," I said, embarrassed. "Your suit is just beautiful."

"It is my favorite," Marco said proudly. "I have two uhzer just like it in different colore, but zees one is best wiz my favorite shoes."

He leaned back on his elbows on the bar and put one foot up on the rail of the stool, posing as if for the cover of *GQ* magazine. I glanced down at his cobalt blue suede penny loafers. Fabulous.

The bartender brought over two glasses of what looked to be champagne, but what Marco explained was a French 75. There was champagne in it, but also gin, simple syrup, and lemon juice. I could only imagine the pukefest and unrelenting hangover that would result from drinking more than a couple of these. I thanked him and drank it though, and before I could order another Murphy's, the bartender sat two more 75s in front of us.

"So, SallEEE, you are free now, eh? 'Ow does it feel?" Marco moved his hand over mine and rubbed the top of it softly with his thumb.

Again . . . inappropriate.

"I'm OK," I said, slipping my hand from under his and picking up my third French 75. "Obviously, it's very different though, going home to an empty house." I arched and stretched, left and right, in a veiled attempt to make sure the coast was clear before adding, "Sleeping alone."

Marco quickly raised and lowered his eyebrows.

"You know I can 'elp wiz zat, SallEEE, at least while you are 'ere."

I played along.

"Come on, Marco," I said, between sips. "What would a young stud like you want with an older gal like me?"

Wait, WHAT did I just SAY?! Frickin' French 75s!

I put down the drink and signaled the bartender for a glass of water. Marco scooted his barstool closer to me and I backed up in response.

"You are not old, SallEEE. I 'ave, shall we say, escorted much older. I prefer mature women; zay are more adventurous. Dey like me to do sings zat zee younger ones are too afraid to try."

Marco winked a knowing wink. I looked at him confused, like I had no idea what he was talking about, but I could imagine.

The bartender sat a glass of water with no ice in front of me and I asked for the check. I drained the glass, hoping to counteract any ensuing damage from those French 75s.

"You are leaving?" Marco asked, surprised, and then directing the bartender to put my beer on his tab.

"Yes, I'm pretty tired actually, but I guess I'll see you here next week?"

"No, no," Marco said. "Just zee first and zee surd Sursdays of zee month. BUT! We are still on for Saturday next, no?"

"Ahh, yes, I guess so . . . um . . . dinner and a party, right?"

"Oui, zat is correct . . . and it is my birdday. I will be surdy-8." He smiled seductively. "You are at Dormir Suites, no?"

"No . . . I mean . . . oui," I said, bumbling, standing up and reaching for my coat.

Marco stood to join me.

"Can I walk you to your 'otel?"

"No thanks, I'm taking a cab."

"OK, SallEEE. Shall we say 7:surdy next Saturday? I will pick you up."

"Yeah, sure Marco, sounds great, and thanks for the beer and the French 75s—I think."

I smiled and he laughed.

"Zay are addictive. Like you, I bet."

"OK, then, I'll see you later," I said, waving, backing up, and turning away before he could do that kiss-kiss thing. I hailed a cab, darted up to my room, and bolted the door.

What was wrong with me? I could have had a piece of that. Isn't that what I said I wanted? A zipless fuck? Why couldn't I go through with it? I promised myself it would be different zee next time.

CHAPTER THIRTEEN

Swinging Boom

The next week flew by with one mini-emergency after the next, hurtling me towards the weekend and my unsettling date with Marco. The thought of getting intimate with him made me anxious, so I tried not to think about it. Instead, whenever I got five minutes to myself, I checked Bill's online status. He was always at work, his status listed as *Available*, but I resisted the urge to ping him. It would only give him hope, and hope is just a tease to keep from accepting reality. He knew it, and that's why he made no attempt to contact me either.

By the time Saturday came, I was at least five pounds thinner. It's actually pretty easy to lose weight when you're really, really, really nervous. I was wearing the same outfit I had worn just two weeks ago at Bill's mom's house, and for the same reasons: besides being flattering, I could get busy in it without taking it off. Why did I wish it was Bill who was on the way over? Sure, Bill could be a little dorky, and the singleness of his fascination with me was a little unnerving, but at least he was a real man. Marco's peacock presentation of his faultless physique accompanied by that heavy accent—it felt affected and cartoonish. And he didn't give one whit about me. I suspected for Marco it was all about the experience and the story.

How ironic.

I poured myself a glass of wine and just then my cell vibrated with a text notification. He was early.

Marco: Room number?

Me: ???

Marco: Party not happening. Drink in room?

So, the little bugger wanted to get it on sooner rather than later. The suspicion this was his plan all along raised my readiness alert level to DEFCON 3. Don't be such a fraidy-cat, I told myself. It's just sex.

I lowered the lighting, flipped on the fireplace, and responded, and shortly thereafter, he was at the door.

"SallEEE!" Marco said, arms wide, holding a dozen red roses and a bottle of Mumm Carte Classique sparkling wine. At about 50 bucks a pop U.S., I was impressed. As for the roses, they're my least favorite: they die too quickly.

This was the first time I had seen Marco dressed down, wearing blue jeans and a red fleece pullover. By comparison, I was overdressed, but I THOUGHT I was going to dinner and a party!

"Lovely," I said, taking the vase and nervously offering my cheek to him. He kissed it and stepped through the door, then held up the champagne.

"May I?" he asked, and I nodded.

Marco do-si-doed to the kitchen, picked up a tea towel, and commenced with the traditional champagne cork removal process, but foam exploded from the bottle. Instinctively, he put his mouth over the top of it, slurping up as much as he could, while some of it bubbled over his hand and spilled into the sink. It conjured thoughts of Bill and the eruption I persuaded from him at his mother's party. The memory was vivid and awash in sound and fury, but it felt long ago and faraway.

I reached for two wine glasses, having no champagne-style ones, and Marco filled them half full with the bubbly. He followed me around the room like a hound onto a fresh scent while I set the roses down here and there, looking for just the right spot. I placed them on the little dining table and turned to face him as he handed me my champagne.

"Santé," he said, tapping his glass against mine and we took our first sip.

"Absolutely delicious, Marco," I said, but wondered if, in a blind tasting, I would be able to tell the difference between it and a far cheaper label. I'm not as discerning with champagne as I am with Sauvignon Blanc.

"Merci, SallEEE. Anysing for you."

And then we stood at the kitchen counter and downed the rest of the bottle. I became a giggling fool, laughing at all of Marco's mispronunciations and malaprops that I suspected he did on purpose to endear himself to female Anglos.

"Do you 'ave any of zee tequila?" Marco asked.

"Do I have any tequila? Well HELL yeah!"

I reached for the spiced honey tequila I brought from Florida and poured a shot in each of our empty wine glasses.

"Try this, dude. No salt and limes necessary—it's the bomb!"

We threw it back simultaneously, then smiled and nodded at each other like, oh yeah, that's the bomb, all right. I couldn't imagine why I had been nervous. Marco was fun!

"SallEEE, can I play some music on zee laptop?"

"Great idea!" I said, stumbling over to the desk and logging in for him.

"Sit down over dare," Marco said, pointing to the couch.

"Wait," I said, "let me get another one of these."

I poured us both a double then teetered over to the couch with bottle in hand.

"OK!" I yelled, "I'm ready! Whaddaya got, Frenchy?!"

For just a moment, Marco appeared to be unsure if I had used Frenchy as a term of endearment or as a shot. I wasn't sure either—it just flew out of mouth, just like it had from my grandfather's all the years I'd known him. Luckily, Marco smiled.

"I have zees for you, SallEEE," he said, cranking the volume as loud as the little laptop could muster. He began head thrusting to the drumbeat of Def Leppard.

"Woohoooo!" I yelled as I rose to join him, but he shook his head and motioned for me to remain on the couch. I thought of Bill at the carriage house: me commanding him to stay put while I did just about the same thing I guessed Marco was about to do.

I threw back the tequila and watched Marco begin to move. It soon became clear that his skill on the dancefloor far outweighed his ability as an engineer. He was crazy sexy, in love with his own body, running one hand under his fleece topper and feeling himself up, while the fingers of his other hand threaded through the satiny curtain of his flaxen hair. He needed no partner; the addition of one would have been superfluous.

Marco boogied his fleece topper off, revealing a white wife-beater clinging to an uber-toned upper body. He swung the fleece around in the air a few times before flinging it towards the wall and accidentally knocked over a lamp. He showed no intention of picking up the lamp, so I staggered over to reposition it. As I wobbled back past him, he squeezed my ass. I looked over my shoulder at him and smiled. I would be telling this story for the rest of my life, and I guessed little embellishment would be necessary.

"Zees is 'ow I paid for university," he said, putting a hand behind his head and rocking his hips, jumping a foot or so towards me with every thrust.

Of course it was, I thought, saluting him with just one more shot of tequila.

"SallEEE, do you like zee Beez Geez?"

"Oh, yes," I said enthusiastically. "Play 'Stayin' Alive'!"

Marco smiled and sipped a little of his tequila, then danced over and grabbed the back of my neck with his meaty paw. He pulled me to him and kissed me on the lips, opening his mouth a little and dribbling some of the tequila into me. Not ready for this alien expression of affection, I lurched forward, spewing some tequila onto my chin.

"Oh, SallEEE, I am so sorry," Marco said with a laugh, slapping me hard on the back and knocking me farther forward towards the carpet. He pulled me up by the back of my dress.

"You will be ready for me next time, eh?"

He kissed me once again. It was soft and tender this time, no tongue and no tequila—no electricity either, but it was an improvement.

Marco began his revival of John Travolta's impressive performance in *Saturday Night Fever*—the striptease was extra. His hand slowly moving up his chest under his wife-beater, exposing what looked like a 14-pack. However, the tequila had a hold on me now, and I was in no condition to be counting. He pulled the wife-beater over his head, then threw it down and jumped on it like it was on fire.

"Go Marco . . . it's your birthday . . . go Marco . . . it's your birthday!!!" I chanted, springing up off the couch, clapping, knowing this would be my best story ever.

WHOAAA! I ducked as one of Marco's loafers flew over my left shoulder as he kicked them off, the other landing on the kitchen counter. And just when I thought it couldn't get any better, he exceeded my expectations, slowly unzipping his fly, sliding his hands down between his jeans and his bright red Speedo briefs with Santa's reindeer on them. WTF? It was only October.

Marco raised his arms up and folded them over his head, grinding and twerking, moving closer to me, his jeans slipping to his knees, beginning to restrain his movement. Then he spun away like a ballerina with her ankles tied together, arms in fifth position. He bent over and yanked the jeans off.

Suddenly, I was sober.

Marco jumped to face me, landing with his legs far apart, then he jerked the front of his Dasher and Dancer's down, releasing his ramburglar. It fired out fast in my direction like a Jack-in-the-Box and landed hard against his leg, just above his kneecap.

THWACK!

I plastered myself against the back of the couch in response, trying to get my impaired mind around it. I knew I wouldn't be able to get my HAND around it, that was for damn sure.

There is big, there is bigger, and then there is Marco, in a class by himself. As he twisted and rocked his hips to the beat, his monster member slapped back and forth against his legs, sort of bending around each thigh.

I flashed back to my teenage years in Canada: my father under the influence, leaning over the side of our sailboat and dipping his glass into the water to add some Lake Erie to his scotch, my mother at the helm, unable to swim but refusing to wear a life jacket, risking her life for a good tan, her fake eyelashes coming loose in the freshwater spray and working their way down her cheeks like skinny caterpillars.

"HARD ALEE!" Dad would shout before the boom would swing to other side of the ship, knocking you ass-over-teakettle if you weren't paying attention.

It was official—Marco would henceforth be known as Swinging Boom.

And then the song was over and another Bee Gees tune faded in. Marco struggled to put his python back in his Prancer and Vixen's, then smoothed his long blond hair back into place and, sensing my apprehension, danced slowly over to me. He placed his hands on my hips and I placed mine on his shoulders and we began to sway to "How Deep is Your Love."

"Why are you wearing Christmas underwear?" I asked, giggling nervously.

"Zay are all I 'ave left from my dancing days. Normally I wear boxers," he answered, smiling seductively, moving his hands around to my lower back, pulling me closer. I reached mine around and up his neck, feeding his hair through my fingers. Silky.

As we moved, we kissed, quietly at first, but then increasingly enthusiastic, until the gentle and soft sounds of the Bee Gees were drowned out by the open, wet, sloppy, gum-sucking.

Marco began slowly working my dress up over my backside and my heart began to pound with uneasy excitement. I could feel his French footlong swelling against me. When he grabbed the hem of the dress with both hands and attempted to pull the garment over my head, I put a stop to it.

"No!" I said sharply, yanking it back down over my hips. "I want to leave it on."

He nodded in understanding, gently rubbing my upper arms. Then he hooked his thumbs under the dress edge where it rested against my collarbone and slowly stretched the flexible fabric under my mondo maracas, exposing their icy tips. He bent down to kiss one and then the other, his fingers making their way between my quivering thighs. He pressed one finger up and through the slit in the crotchless lace, tickling my entrance. Then he snaked it around the fabric and tugged. He kissed my neck and whispered in my ear.

"OK cherie, we will do it your way, but I am going to take off zee panties. I cannot fit tru zee 'ole."

Marco lowered himself to his knees and slipped off my stilettos, reciting "This Little Piggy" as he wiggled each toe in succession. I struggled to maintain my balance during this bizarre interlude. It's all about the story, I kept telling myself. Finally, he ran his hands up the back of my legs and slowly dragged my panties down to my ankles with his curiously long nails. Shiver.

"Are you cold, SallEEE?"

"Ah . . . no . . . I think I'm a little nervous," I said.

Marco stood and hugged me.

"Lie down," he said. "Close your eyes. I have just zee sing to 'elp."

I climbed onto the bed and barely shut my eyes, peering through the tiny slits in an effort to prepare myself for Marco's next move. He got onto the bed with me, then turned and laid down facing the opposite direction, 69-style. I imagined myself choking to death. He began massaging my foot, rubbing the ball of it, pushing into the instep. It felt pretty good. But as soon as I started to relax, Marco took weird up a notch and swung his leg over my waist, sitting on me reverse cowgirl. Then he bent over and started massaging both of my feet, licking and sucking the big toes. He made an mmmmmm sound, like he was tasting something yummy.

When he'd had his fill, he bounced off and lay down beside me like a normal person. I rolled to face him and he lifted my leg over his waist. He smiled as he reached, once again, between my resistive thighs.

"Zat did not get you hot, eh SallEEE?"

"Sorry. I guess feet don't really do it for me. It was a new experience though," I said apologetically, appreciating the effort, no matter how surreal. Marco brushed my cheek with the back of his hand, his amber eyes sparkling.

"Marco sinks you want zee real sing," he said, his lips curling around the words.

My God he was beautiful. Why did he have to crazy everything up? And why, all of a sudden, was he referring to himself in the third person?

He got off the bed and, still in performance mode, looked over his shoulder at me as he bent forward and inched his Comet and Cupid's down, his big balls dropping half a foot. When he spun to face me, I almost yelled HARD ALEE! as his semi-erect Johnson swung violently across his body. He fetched it before it got away from him and then stroked it, smiling. I wished I was back at the Orlando Grand Tropics watching Bill stroke his relatively deficient appendage. And then I remembered something.

"Wait!" I said, pointing to the bedside table. Marco nodded like he knew what I wanted and opened the small drawer. He ripped open a Magnum and struggled to get it on, then climbed onto the bed, his hefty pecker pointing due south like a jack hammer about to drill through concrete.

Marco laid down on top of me, his crotch cannon trespassing between us like an unwanted guest. He kneaded my nippers with his right hand while his other worked the dress above my hips. His legs prodded mine apart. Then he was back up on his knees, stroking himself. I saw the concern on his face, and it increased my anxiety.

"We are going to need zee lube, SallEEE," he said, matter-a-fact, shrugging his shoulders.

"I don't have any," I said. "What about cocoa butter, will that work?" I pointed to the bathroom.

"Aha! Yes, you ladies do love zee cocoa butter!" Marco jumped to his feet and bounced on the bed a few times before flying through the bathroom door like Peter Pan, his tenderloin of beef swinging up and around counter-clockwise. I wondered if it would circle around the other way if we were in the southern hemisphere.

He held the cocoa butter up, pointing to it and nodding as he rotated his hips, and his dancing sirloin bounced to the beat. Then he squirted the moisturizer on his hand and lay down beside me once again. I pitched my hips against his prodding fingers like I was really enjoying his touch, trying to convince him, but mostly myself, that I wanted this.

"Zees might be a little uncomfortable, SallEEE, but I promise, after a few more times wiz Marco, you will not be satisfied wiz anysing less. I will ruin you for any uhzer man."

I knew he didn't mean it the way I took it, which was to imagine an average-sized fellow feeling like he was bonking a bucket of soapy water. I committed then and there to 100 Kegel squeezes per day for the rest of my life.

We worked together on the Get Zees Big Sing in Zare project: Marco spreading cocoa butter on us like cream cheese on a bagel, until the bottle was almost empty and he had approximately 80 percent penetration. At that point, we relaxed a little, giggling and kissing, trying to get some semblance of normalcy back into the act. Unfortunately, he was a sloppy kisser, going after my face like a thirsty dog. I jerked my head around, chasing his tongue, trying to keep it in my mouth, but eventually gave up and turned my head sideways. As his humping accelerated, he moved his mouth to my ear and murmured a mix of French and English nonsense.

"Je comprends zee ladies . . . voulez-vous dick?"

Marco moved his arms under my legs, lifting my hips, watching himself perform the push-and-pull.

Then he raised his gaze to look at me—his upper body flexed and shiny as if in a bodybuilding competition, his hair swinging and sticking to his beautifully carved face. I softened and miraculously took in the last 20 percent of him, and as he did his best to make the evening worth my while, I crossed that threshold where I knew I could climax.

"Oh yeah," I groaned. "That's it . . . uh . . . oh God. I'm feeling . . . good now."

"Ahhh, SallEEE," he whispered with confidence as he lowered himself onto me, tunneling deeper into me. "You love my big boNER buried in your pussEEE. Tell me you do."

"God yes I DO! Give it to me! Here I go . . . here I go . . . oh God give it all to me, BILL!"

SHAZAM!

It was nice. Not the best orgasm, but hey, it was a bona fide orgasm. As for the journey itself—too frickin' weird. I was glad it was over. I wilted back against the mattress and smiled up at Marco. He didn't smile back. His expression intensified; his eyes narrowed.

"And now it is my turn, SallEEE," he said, sitting back on his knees and rolling the rubber off. He threw it on the floor and after struggling to get the last bit of cocoa butter out of the bottle, he threw the bottle after it.

What the hell?

I sat up and scooted back against the headboard, confused. Marco followed, straddling me, his legs on either side of my hips pinning me in place. He passed his lubricated palm along his unwrapped semi-stiffness, then raised his eyes to meet mine.

"I am going to come on you, SallEEE . . . watch me . . . show me you want it . . . come on cherie . . . show me," he said, rocking up and down on my thighs, stroking himself with increasing speed and ferocity, his moby dick just a couple inches away from my face and neck.

"Grab my ass, SallEEE, squeeze it! Marco is going to open fire on your face. Get ready, SallEEE, AHHHH! OHHHH! Stick out your tongue, cherie, stick out your TONGUE!"

I couldn't remember feeling as helpless as I did at that moment. I wanted to be anywhere but there, about to get a faceful of Marco's high fructose porn syrup.

"Marco, wait!" I said, pleading with him. "Slow down."

I pushed on his thighs, trying to stop the exuberant bouncing, but he continued, leaning forward, putting his tip against my neck. He was seconds away.

"Ahhhhh, yessssss, are you ready for Marco, are you READY?! AH . . . AH . . . AH . . . OHHHHH!"

I turned my head and semen shot into my ear.

Marco grabbed the scruff of my neck and pulled my head forward, releasing into my hair, and then he pressed his porksicle against my pursed lips.

"OUI . . . OUI . . . OUI!!!" he squealed, like a little kid on a swing as his purple turkey baster breached the perimeter and painted my teeth with his last few drops.

Marco jumped off the bed and strutted around the room, his jumbo Johnson hanging long and low, getting tangled up with his legs, almost tripping him.

"YES!" he exclaimed, pumping his fist in the air. "That was good, SallEEE! You make me give you a lot of my essence."

Marco did a couple hip thrusts in my direction and then a pirouette, as if the screwing had been part of the performance and now it was time to return to the dance. Then he stopped abruptly, found his clothes, and put them on.

"SallEEE, I am sinking Tim 'ortons. Panini or a wrap, per'aps?" he asked, rescuing his wayward loafers and slipping them on.

I was still in shock, covered in semen, and unable to hear out of my left ear.

"Did you say Tim Hortons?"

"I admit, SallEEE, I am addicted to zare food and coffee, just like all Canadiens," Marco said, distracted now, looking for his keys.

"You know, Marco, it's been great, really, but I'm pretty tired after all the excitement, and I'd have to have a shower, and well . . ."

"OK cherie, I can take zee 'int." He smiled broadly, picking his keys up off the desk. "You ladies want Marco for his body, and zen you want to return to your routine. Je comprends. I will see you at Flanagan's on Sursday, no?"

"Sure," I said, shaken but relieved the show was finally over.

Marco took a bow and exited stage right.

CHAPTER FOURTEEN

Why Don't You Call Him?

I bolted the door behind Marco and walked back into the bedroom to survey the carnage. The mangled bedding was covered in greasy stains, presumably from the cocoa butter. I didn't see any of Marco's essence, as he called it, probably because I was wearing all of it.

And about that dress. I'd worn it only twice, and twice had been regretful upon removing it. Gingerly, I pulled the tacky, albeit flattering frock over my head and stuffed it in the kitchen trash. Anxious to remove any further traces of Marco's DNA, I headed for the shower and as I did, the unwelcome surprise of the used Magnum saran-wrapped my bare foot. I peeled it away with the tips of my fingernails and held the empty sack up and away from my body. It looked like a well-worn knee-hi stocking. While the shower heated, I gargled with mouthwash then brushed my teeth. Was it my imagination or were they whiter?

Nah, that's just urban legend.

"May I help you?" asked the helpful-sounding woman at the other end of the phone line.

"Yes. Can you have a complete set of bedding, including pillows, sent to my room?"

"Is anything wrong with the bedding, madam?"

"Yes, but it isn't your fault. I'm afraid I've made a bit of a mess. I'll change the bedding myself."

"Ah, oui, that is no problem, madam. Is there anything else I can do for you?"

"Yes. Can you transfer me to room service please?"

I ordered my usual: cheeseburger, medium, mustard, mayo, tomato, onion, and pickles, no lettuce.

"Take what you like, madam," the bellboy said, craning his scrawny neck to peer over my shoulder into the room, trying to discern what event could have precipitated the unusual request.

"Thank you so much," I said, embarrassed as I pulled clean bedding from the laundry cart plus a few extra towels.

"Can you take that with you?" I asked, arms full, kicking at the heap of dirty linens on the floor next to the door.

"Ahhh," he said hesitating, then, "Oui, of course."

He picked up the pile, angling his head as far back and away from it as he could, then dumped it in a laundry bag attached to the cart. Then he turned and rolled the cart down the hall towards the elevator.

While I waited for my supper, I opened my laptop and recorded the loony particulars of the evening's zipless adventure, focusing only on the what. Feeling much improved after having eaten, I reclined on the couch to reflect on the why. Why had I done the devil's dance with Marco? To be sure, it was an alcohol-related incident, but I knew before I even got on the plane that I was going to do it, even though my gut told me it was wrong. Having decided the best course of action was to forget about it until it was time to narrate it, I closed my eyes. Unintentionally,

I tumbled into an unsettling dream.

I was sailing on the rough seas of Lake Erie with Bill. He was at the bow of the ship, holding onto the forestay. At first glance, he looked like a naked Ken-doll, his golden chest disproportionately broad, his anatomically incorrect pelvis slight by comparison. His cowboy hat appeared to be glued to his head, as the wind and pitch tried in vain to blow it off him. I raised my hand to shield my eyes and squinted across the length of the ship to focus, and I noticed he was indeed wearing a bathing suit. It was a skin-tone, skin-tight Speedo that suggested there wasn't much under the fabric. He was waving and pointing to something behind me. I turned to look at the wheel: it was rotating right, then left, then right, then harder right, then left again, attempting to keep on course, but there was no one at the helm. I looked back at Bill, confused, squinting again, bringing him back into focus, and saw his lips form the words, HARD ALEE!

By the time the actual sound traveled from his mouth over the howl of the wind and flap of the sails, it was too late. I turned just in time to see the boom swing hard into me, knocking the air out of my lungs, batting me over the side and into the turbulent water.

Down, down, under the wild waves I went, the Comfy Janes housecoat forced up, encircling my arms and face, hampering my ability to stay afloat. Panic. I ripped the snaps open and the current tore the old robe from me. Struggling to reach the surface, I finally breached it, fighting for air. Bitch-slapped by the roll of the next wave, I filled with lake water.

A last gasp for oxygen propelled me to consciousness and an upright seated position. Disoriented and in a cold sweat, I soon became aware of my surroundings, and then I remembered what had taken place there that evening. I picked up my cell and started to text him.

Me: Bill can we talk?

My finger hovered over the Send button, just briefly, before I came to my senses.

Yes, I missed him, and the dream, it felt like a sign. But nothing had really changed, except that I had invited a crazy French Canadian into my bed just to prove I could. Just for the experience. Just for the story.

I made the bed, crawled into it, and prayed for sleep without dreams.

It was Sunday. Today would be a good day to visit the Notre Dame Basilica and go to mass. I had fallen away from that practice since Lance had left me, as he was the one who was strict about attendance. But all that church-going hadn't prevented him from destroying our marriage. I realized I had used his weakness as an excuse to stop going myself, but the church bells came and went, and along with it, my resolve to go.

Instead, I picked up my phone.

"It's about time you called," Laura said. "I was getting worried. What are you doing?"

"Right now? Kegel exercises."

"What?"

I couldn't help myself. I went straight to Swinging Boom. Listening to her react—hooting, hollering, and laughing—made the living through it, almost worth it.

"You have GOT to be making that shit up, Sally. Come on! I know you're exaggerating his size—you HAVE to be. And the reindeer underwear? Admit it."

"I swear on my mother's life, Laura, it's all true."

"You know you aren't safe to let out. He could have killed you! He sounds certifiable."

"Nah, I've known him for years; he's harmless. But you're right. It was a mistake," I said, finally feeling the weight of that mistake upon hearing the word.

"So, not to change the subject, but have you heard from Bill?"

"Bill? No, not since I got here," I said, caught off guard by Laura's innocent attempt to obtain classified material. "Why do you ask?"

"Just kind of sad you two aren't seeing each other anymore. I mean, the way you described that passion and intensity." She sighed longingly. "Anyway, you always make me feel like my life is so boring. You have to tell me the Swinging Boom story again, in person, as soon as you get back here."

"OK friend. See you in two weeks."

Unexpectedly and unfortunately, Marco was in the office Monday, rather than in the field with the techs. And although we both knew it was just a zipless, albeit an extremely strange one, interacting with him was awkward. When I said hi, he winked. When he passed me in the hall, he brushed his hand across my back, pretending he needed to squeeze by. At the coffee bar, he bit into a French pastry and cheese oozed onto his chin. He shot me a seductive look as he coaxed the creamy goodness into his mouth with his meandering tongue.

I wanted to rewind my life.

"Craig Chester, Operations."

"Bonjour," I said mysteriously into the phone.

"Hey, what's happening Sally?!"

"Just checking up on my boys," I said. "Everything under control down there?"

"Yep. Brian's running the staff meeting this morning. I'll lead the afternoon session. It's been quiet. So, you wowing 'em up there in Oh Canada?"

"You know it started it out pretty good," I said, "but there's been so much input and revision to my original proposal, even if the outcome is wildly successful, it's doubtful I'll get the credit."

"Well, at least you got a trip to Montreal out of it," Craig said.

"That's true. It's getting pretty chilly though," I said, a twinge of gloom darkening my spirit at the thought of staying much longer, considering things had not gone as planned. "OK, well I don't want to keep you."

"Oh wait!" Craig interjected, "I almost forgot. So, that guy you felt up at Rogers Park."

Craig chuckled.

"Haha very funny," I said, but Craig's teaser had incited a surge of adrenaline. "What about him?"

"He and his family made the November issue of the *SEA Family Newsletter*," Craig said. "Something about turtles. Standby. I'll email you the link."

I opened the link and scrolled down to the grainy and poorly composed photograph. It looked like it had been taken from the wooden bridge behind the Pruitt family compound in Sundown Beach. Bill's family were marking sea turtle nests.

"Yeah, that's Bill and his younger brothers, Johnny and Doug. The redhead is his sister Rosie, and the woman with the signpost is his sister-in-law Deb. I have no idea who the—"

"Well, well, well," said Craig, interrupting me. "So you met his family."

Oops.

"Good!" he said, surprising me. "Because I'm hoping you can get me the 4-1-1 on the danger kitty in the Rio cut bikini. Is that Bill's daughter?"

Standing almost directly in front of Bill and with her back to the camera was the undeniable focus of the amateur composition, the only one who wasn't fully clothed, which was strange considering the gray, gusty day advertised in the image. Her face was tilted skyward and her elbows spread wide and high as she attempted to corral her long black wind-blown tresses. Bill was waving at the camera but his eyes were on her.

"I've never seen her before," I said, feigning dis-interest, "and I don't know if Bill has any children."

"You two don't talk much when you're together, do you." Craig laughed. "Anyway, I think this is the most read company newsletter ever. I've seen this picture on more than one monitor today and it's not because the guys give a damn about sea turtles."

"Well, sorry I couldn't be of any help, Craig," I said, unsettled by the outside possibility this provoc-ative interloper was romantically involved with Bill.

"OK Sally, and hey, I want to hear the How-I-Met-Your-Mother story or whatever you're calling it, as soon as you get back here."

Thirsty Thursday rolled around again, and I made my way to Flanagan's with some coworkers. We sat at the bar and quickly moved past work-talk and onto more interesting topics. Some of the men my age were very handsome and accomplished, but of course, they were all attached. Suddenly, Bill stormed my psyche along with the svelte family photobomber on the beach. The way he looked at her; there was something there.

After a couple of Guinness, nature called and I excused myself to go to the restroom. I couldn't find it. I have no sense of direction, and Flanagan's dark labyrinth of narrow stairs and curved hallways confused me. I rounded an unfamiliar corner and unexpectedly caught a glimpse of Marco and Desirée. His back was to me and he was pressing her up against the stone wall with his torso, whispering in her ear. She was laughing. Then she turned her head in my direction and his followed. I stepped back around the corner and out of sight.

"SallEEE?" Marco said.

Shit.

"Hi," I said, waving as I walked towards them. "Don't mind me, I'm lost as usual. I'm looking for the bathroom."

"It is on zee uhzer side of zee bar." Marco smiled and approached. "SallEEE, do you remember my assistant, Desirée DanNER?"

"Yes, of course," I said, shaking her hand. "How are you, Desirée?"

"I am well, merci."

"I was telling Desirée what fun you and I 'ad Saturday." Marco winked a mischievous wink. "I sink we sree should get togezer."

Desirée ran her hands up and down my arms.

"'ow about tonight, SallEEE, after 'appy hour? We could go to your 'otel," she said suggestively.

"Ummmm, gee, that would have been great, but I'm afraid I have other plans," I said, feigning disappointment. "I'll have to take a rain check. Right now, I need to find that bathroom."

I whisked away from them tout suite. If I wasn't mistaken, they had just propositioned me with a ménage à trois—more commonly known in the good ol' U.S. of A. as a threesome. I imagined them jumping on the bed naked, Desirée spiraling down towards the mattress, her perky breasts lifting to meet her chin, her long brown hair floating above her. Marco rising next to her, his man-pipe swinging down between his legs, whip-slapping his ass under his balls. Then I tried to imagine myself bouncing between them.

No, I can't imagine it either.

There was a long line at the ladies room, so by the time I got back to the bar almost everyone from work had left. I put on my coat and prepared to leave. Then I heard a voice behind me.

"'oo is Bill?"

I turned to face Marco.

"What are you talking about?"

"Is 'ee your ex-'usband?"

"No."

"Is 'ee your loVER?"

"No!"

Marco grabbed my arm and pulled me closer, then put his mouth to my ear.

"Oh God give it all to me, BILL!" Marco mimicked, perfectly unfrenchified. Then he let go of me and stepped back.

"I believe zose were zee exact words."

My knees weakened a little and I looked away, trying to compose myself.

Marco softened.

"I did not know if you knew you said it, and clearly you did not. You want zees Bill, no?"

"No," I whispered. "I mean . . . maybe . . . I don't know."

"I sink you do. I sink you are trying to be someone zat you are not."

"I appreciate your concern, Marco," I said guardedly. "Just please don't mention our evening together to anyone else."

"Of course, SallEEE, bon chance," he said with an understanding nod and strutted away, his silver gray suit jacket flapping side to side.

I stepped out into the cool evening wind and hoofed it to my hotel, and once inside, diverted to the hotel bar. I laid claim to a seat in a row of empty ones and ordered a gin and soda. A distinguished looking older gentleman at the far end of the bar raised his glass to me, and I saluted him with mine. We being the only two patrons, I wasn't surprised when he rose to join me.

He was 75 years old and, just by coincidence, was passing through Montreal on what would have been his 50th anniversary. He had lost his wife two years previous—they had been married at the Basilica. His name was Ron Beaver, and he was from Buffalo.

"Beaver?" I said with a grin. "I'm guessing you took quite a bit of ribbing growing up with that name."

"It's even better than you think," he said, leaning in close, his watery brown eyes smiling. "I had horrible teeth, but didn't manage to get braces until much later in life, and by then the nickname had stuck. Everyone calls me Bucky."

"Bucky Beaver?!"

He pulled a card from his wallet and passed it to me.

The card read *Ron "Bucky" Beaver, Prosthodontist.*

"You make dentures?" I asked, slapping the bar with a hoot.

"Not anymore. I'm retired now. But I've still got two boxes of the cards."

"Bucky, you just made my day."

"Now you tell me something about yourself," Bucky said, and I wasted no time reciting the Lance Pants Down tale, ending with my declaration to never be monogamous again. Then, somewhat sadly, I added a little about Bill and his unwillingness to play by my rules.

"Ah . . . friends with benefits. That's a young man's game," Bucky said, sipping his wine. "And not very satisfying, even for a young man."

I changed the subject. "So, have you found someone else?"

"I think maybe I have. She's wonderful and beautiful—considerably younger."

"Of course she is," I said dryly.

I was sure Bucky had thrown in the age disparity disclosure just so he could address it, which I found odd considering I had just told him my ex-husband had blown up our family to get that same sad, stereotypical arrangement.

"Look, I didn't seek her out!" he began to explain in earnest. "She pursued me. Despite the age difference, we do have a lot in common, plus she needs the financial stability I provide. I don't mind the compromise. I don't want to be alone."

It was quiet for a moment as we sipped our drinks, and then he continued.

"You know, Sally, it's going to be difficult to find someone willing to put up with your arrangement. Any man worth anything won't do it. Now, why don't you call him?"

"Call who," I asked facetiously.

"The man who loves you," Bucky said. "I'm going to turn in, but I want to hear what happens. You have my card."

He signed his tab then got up to leave.

"Great meeting you, Bucky," I said, shaking his hand, "and I promise I'll email you with the rest of the story as soon as I know how it ends."

Back in my room, I sat down at the desk and opened my laptop. Bill was online, obviously working late. I thought maybe I should ping him at work instead of texting his cell.

Oh what the hell difference would that make! Get ON with it, girl!

I pulled my phone from my purse and stared at the unsent text.

Me: Bill can we talk?

Just as I was about to press Send, my cell rang. I was so on edge, the noise and vibration startled me, and I jerked my arm up, launching the phone from my hand. It tumbled under the coffee table. By the time I was able to fetch it, the ringing had stopped. I touched to see who had called. It was Bill.

I jumped with excitement. All these days incommunicado . . . and I meet a stranger who tells me to call Bill . . . and Bill calls me at exactly the same time I'm about to text him! It couldn't be a coincidence! Surely, it was a sign!

I jumped again when a voicemail notification popped.

"Ah, hey Sally, it's Bill. Was just thinking about you, wondering how you are doing up there in the great white north. I'm in Burlington, not too far away actually . . . ah . . . OK then . . . have a great weekend."

I started pacing the floor, the gears in my mind grinding out an appropriate response. I would call back, definitely call back, but how would I play it?

Does this game come with instructions?

"Hi Sally, thanks for calling," Bill said, sounding surprised.

"Hi stranger. Didn't think I'd hear from you again," I replied, coolly of course. "Ummm, Burlington?"

"Vermont. Don't you remember? I'm working on a problem with one of our contractors. I've been up here all week. I thought it silly not to call . . . you know . . . when I'm this close."

"When do you go back?" I asked, just making friendly small talk but wondering how long he'd be around.

"Day after tomorrow. Guess you'll be up there another week or so. Are you enjoying yourself?"

"Actually, I'm a little homesick, not sure why," I said, slipping into wistfulness. "Too bad you have to leave Saturday. You could have come up for the weekend. We could have—"

I bit my bottom lip to stop myself, unsure of the direction I had just swung the conversation in.

"Ummm . . . well . . . I could . . . I think. I just have to get my flight changed to Monday. Would that work for you?" he asked, tentatively.

Hesitation.

"Sure, that'll work, but you need a passport to cross

the border. I'm sure you don't have that with you," I said, my heart beginning to beat hard at the realization he may soon be within arm's reach—literally.

"Yeah, I have it. I mean . . . you never know," Bill said happily. "Gee, this is great, Sally. I haven't been to Montreal since I was a teenager. Shall we say 3 o'clock? We'll have some drinks and I'll take you to dinner."

"Sounds good," I replied matter-a-fact, like no big deal, but I didn't sleep all night.

CHAPTER FIFTEEN

B.H.R.T

It was 4 pm; he was an hour late. I opened the fridge and stared at the unopened bottle of Sauvignon Blanc, but determined to wait for him before celebrating, I closed the door and walked back into the bedroom to gauge my appearance in the full-length mirror. The fitted black pantsuit with flared bottoms and cutout shoulders was slimming and just a little bit sexy. The black and white cowboy boots added a fun factor that would tip off any onlookers that I wasn't from around here—not sure why I bothered pulling them on, though. I'd have the bottom half of this outfit off before Bill could say, How's yer father?

Tired of wandering aimlessly in search of something to rearrange, I decided to lie down. Stretched out on the bed, I raised my left arm and admired my wedding ring: so beautiful, so familiar, so part of my life for so long, like an old friend. I still wore it often, usually on my right hand, but that evening I was wearing it as it should be worn. Was I trying to send Bill a message? If so, it would be a confusing one. After all, I was only interested in a physical commitment from Bill.

Did someone just call bullshit?

And then a text.

Bill: I'm at the bar

Me: Room 531

Bill: Come down i'm taking you to dinner

Me: No come up i'm taking you to bed ;)

Bill: No

WTF? Supper before sex? I slipped some mints and anti-gas chewables into my silver purse and then grabbed my coat and walked to the elevator. Alone in that small space, charged and anxious, I watched the numbers slowly decrement from 5 to L.

I scanned the crowded room, then I caught sight of him. Like me, Bill was obviously not from around here, his golden tan even more pronounced against the peek of his white tee from under his butter-colored v-neck sweater. When our eyes met, his smile illuminated the dimly lit space like a match struck in a dark room. The crowd of patrons in his orbit faded to gray in contrast. And at that moment, I wondered if everyone saw him as I did: by far and away the most magnetic man in the room.

I wormed my way through the mob to reach him and we hugged. Rising on tippy toes, I reached for the back of his neck and whispered in his ear, "I've missed you."

He hugged me tighter. All was well.

"Here, you sit down," he said, sliding off the stool. "I've been in the car for hours."

I grabbed the counter for support and he pushed the stool under me. Then he raised his hand to get the bartender's attention, and very quickly I had a gin and soda in my hand.

"What took you so long?" I asked, not really caring what the answer was. I just wanted to listen to him and look at him. Such an attractive man, but either unaware of it or unaffected by it—so very different than Marco. Marco was sexy, more than handsome, and overconfident, more than comfortable in his own skin.

I nursed my drink while Bill described his experience at the Highgate Springs border crossing. To make his long story short, both the line of cars and the interrogations had been lengthier than anticipated. And then the talking stopped and we were just sipping our drinks, grinning at one another through the din of busy bar background noise.

"So, you missed me," he said, breaking the silence between us. "You know I've been thinking about you ever since that night at Mom's. I hated the way that ended."

He looked down at his beer, pensive now. I didn't interrupt.

"It took all my courage to call you Thursday night, but I had to at least hear your voice one more time. I was very surprised you invited me up."

He smiled a little before raising his glass.

"Now, don't go all serious on me, Bill," I said, wagging my finger at him. "I had an ulterior motive when I invited you up here."

I swept my palm across his thigh, then squeezed the inside of his leg, apparently a little too close for comfort. He twisted away.

"Sally . . . ah . . . I don't want to spoil your fun, but could we just enjoy the evening without the pressure to . . . I mean . . . I just got here."

I laughed.

"You're acting like a young girl on a first date, Bill."

"Well, you're acting like a . . ."

My eyes widened waiting for him to finish the sentence.

"Jesus, look at the time!" he blurted out. "Our dinner reservations are in five minutes."

He rushed to help me on with my coat and steered me out of the bar and into the brisk night air.

"Where are we going?" I asked, peeved that my initial overture had been rebuked.

Bill took my hand, interlacing his fingers with mine, and then walked me across the street.

"La Vie," he responded.

La Vie is a wine and jazz bar only a seven minute walk from the hotel. It's easily identified by bright yellow awnings hanging over an attractive sidewalk terrace. Immediately upon entering, we were welcomed by Julien, the owner, who led us through the crowded restaurant. The French-inspired decor was complete with dark wood against stone walls, which were decorated with towering posters. An iron staircase led to the second floor from which live jazz flowed throughout the interior. Despite being expansive and spread over three floors, the sophisticated space still felt cozy and romantic. We rounded a corner and took our seat in a quiet nook.

"Great choice," I said, absorbing the ambiance.

"Bonjour, hello," the waitress said, which was customary in Montreal. Depending on the response, she would know whether to speak French or English.

"Hello," said Bill, before I could say bonjour and make a fool of myself. I remember very little French from high school. I ordered a gin and soda, and Bill ordered a draft Carlsberg. The waitress disappeared and we perused the menu, which was small but interesting. Like most menus in Montreal, it was French on one side and English on the other.

"Would you be interested in just splitting some appetizers?" I asked. "I don't want too much food."

"Sure, what looks good to you?"

"You do," I said smiling, rubbing the inside of his leg again, but down closer to the knee this time.

"Settle down girl," he said with a grin.

That brought back memories. Lance used to say the same thing and for the same reason.

"Braised lamb poutine sounds brilliant," I said, pointing to it on the menu.

"What's poutine?"

I looked at him like he was from Planet Claire.

"It's ONLY the national dish of Canada," I said,

excited to describe it. "The original version from Quebec is French fries covered with cheddar cheese curds, then smothered in gravy. It's typically beef gravy, but in the Maritime Provinces, they use chicken gravy. Everyone everywhere makes it now, and they've gotten pretty creative with it."

"Sounds heavy," said Bill, unimpressed, "and I'm not sure I like lamb."

"Oh my God, Bill, who doesn't like lamb?" I said incredulously, although my own father couldn't even stand the smell of it cooking.

"OK," Bill said, somewhat begrudgingly, "but can we start with this salad? It has candied walnuts on it."

Oh brother.

Once the salad arrived, we each ordered a glass of Chateau St. Jean Cabernet Sauvignon from Napa.

"Is that your wedding ring?" Bill asked, holding my hand lightly in his and rolling the ring around my finger, being careful not to smudge the full carat diamond.

I nodded.

"It's beautiful. Do you . . . want people to think . . . you're married?" he asked, furrowing his brows.

"I wear it sometimes," I said nostalgically, not answering his question.

I can be so annoying.

The poutine came and we made small talk while we shared the two plates, moving our forks back and forth between them. The salad was perfect. Bill gnawed on the lettuce and walnuts, and I ate the beets and goat cheese that he had pushed to the side. The lamb poutine was amazing, and although he tried not to like it, I could tell Bill, picky as he was, would eventually become a poutine fan, just like everyone else.

We ordered a second glass of wine, and the waitress took the empty plates away. Figuring this would be as good a time as any, I started up what I knew would be a sensitive topic.

"So, when we were at Rogers Park, my boss told me about you and Jane."

Bill's face fell.

"He and some others saw us walking to your van, and apparently they got concerned. Was just wondering if I could get your side of the story."

I squeezed his hand in encouragement.

Just then, the waitress placed the wine in front of us. Bill peered into the glass of garnet liquid as if it was a crystal ball about to reveal something of a helpful nature. Resigned, he took a five dollar gulp and commenced with his heartbreak autobiography.

Bill and Dana had been in love since high school and never apart for any length of time. Trying for years to have children, they finally gave up the dream when, before they knew it, they were in their forties and the children had never come. Bill thought the absence of children had made them closer—they only had each other. I've always thought the opposite was true, but I didn't interject my opinion.

Jane Yarburg was his administrative assistant. She and her husband, Randy, had been good friends with Bill and Dana for many years. The foursome played golf together, went on vacations together, and met each week for happy hour. And then by a bizarre coincidence, Randy was killed in a car crash on the same day Dana passed away from breast cancer.

Not surprisingly, Bill and Jane grieved together, but as time went by, Jane got over her despair somewhat and wanted a life less constrained by sadness. Bill, however, was unable to move on. He needed professional counseling, but instead had relied totally on Jane for emotional support. Then one day, that need turned physical.

"She brought some papers into my office for me to sign, and I tried to kiss her."

Bill looked down, averting my eyes, before continuing.

"There was a bit of a struggle. She said no and asked me to stop, but I persisted."

"Holy shit!" I blurted out, surprised by Bill's confession, although I'd been forewarned by Mark. I leaned in and brought my voice down.

"So that's why she filed a sexual harassment suit against you."

"Not true," Bill said, surprising me once again. "My office door was open, and Ruth Crowley, another admin, heard us and came in just in time to see me in the worst possible light. She demanded to know what was going on. Jane tried to calm her down in an effort to protect me, but Ruth contacted her Ethics Adviser, and the episode was escalated."

"I'm sorry, Bill," I said sincerely. "But GEEZ man, what would you expect?"

Bill took a ten dollar gulp of his wine, and it was gone.

"Jane was forced to admit what happened, and I was suspended without pay for three months while a proper investigation could be conducted. I was sure I'd be fired, so I put my condo on the market and moved back in with Mom. I'm down at her place all the time anyway. I lined up a job with a small engineering law firm there in Sundown, but when they found out about the situation at SEA, they made the job contingent on my name being cleared. In the end, I wasn't fired, but I'm sure I would have been if Jane hadn't continued to argue on my behalf. She told them it was partly her fault, that maybe she had given me the wrong idea and led me on. That wasn't true, of course, but it shows you what kind of woman and friend she is."

"Yes, it does," I said, doing a 180 on my attitude towards Comfy Jane. "But why didn't you take the job in Sundown?"

"I intended to. But after some time in counseling, I realized I wouldn't be happy until I went back to SEA and proved I wasn't a complete nut job. So, I took my condo off the market and returned to work. It was rough those first few months, lots of whispering in the halls. Not just because they knew what I'd done, but because I hadn't paid the ultimate price. The fact that I was a SEA attorney made it worse; if anyone should have known better, it should have been me. That's why I put in for the Program Management job and I'm guessing that's why I got it—different title, different location, different team."

Bill looked down at the table and began to sweep breadcrumbs into a pile with the edge of his hand. To be sure, it had been important to hear his story, but man-oh-man was it a downer. I needed to turn this dateship around before it sailed off the edge of the earth, but before I could detour the conversation, Bill looked up from his employment and continued his explanation.

"You know, at the time it didn't feel like I was doing anything wrong. I mean, Jane and I had a relationship outside of work—we were close, very close. But looking back on it now, I understand how serious it was, and it certainly was grounds for firing. That's why the rumors started about my family paying Jane off, which never happened. Everything she did for me was out of friendship. I didn't see her much after that because I went to Riverview and she transferred to the Briny Bay branch. Shortly after that, she retired."

"Damn, Bill," I said, "that's one helluva story—although it could be better. I'd amp up the struggle scene if I was narrating it."

I grinned and rubbed his shoulder, but he recoiled in response.

"NARRATE IT?! I don't even want to REMEMBER it!"

"Ah, sorry," I said. "I didn't mean to . . . anyway, you got lucky. Not only didn't you get fired, you got a promotion. And Jane is still your friend."

"True," Bill said, cautiously, "except for my reputation, which obviously hasn't recovered, otherwise your boss wouldn't have been concerned to see you with me . . . Sally, can we change the subject?"

"You read my mind," I said.

"Can we talk about you . . . and . . . um . . ." He leaned in closer. "Sex."

"My favorite subject," I said. "Especially when you're around."

"It's just that . . . that . . . well . . . I mean . . . most women your . . ."

"Age." I finished it for him.

"Yes . . . age. You're different . . . you seem a little preoccupied . . . with . . . with . . ."

"For God's sake Bill, spit it out!"

"With IT!" he exclaimed. "You're a cougar, aren't you?"

"I am NOT a COUGAR!"

Heads turned our way, accompanied by some raised eyebrows and snickers.

Turns out the French word for cougar, is cougar.

Bill turned as red as the beets I had eaten. I lowered my voice to a whisper and gave him a playful push.

"Oh my God, Bill. How the hell did you get to be 52 years old without knowing what poutine is or what a cougar is? A cougar is an older woman that seeks sex with younger men. I'm not after youth. I'm looking for experience."

Just then, Swinging Boom's 38 year-old face flashed before me, somewhat belaying what I had just forcefully declared, but I raised my wine glass and clinked it against Bill's empty one.

"You're almost too young for me, Bill." I winked and took a sip.

He appeared to be unsatisfied with my thin response.

"You're right, though," I continued more seriously, "I do think about sex a lot. There's a good reason for that. Shall I explain?"

"Please do," Bill answered, but the look on his face conveyed something very different, like he wasn't quite sure this was a mystery he wanted to solve.

"A year before I caught Lance in bed with what's-her-name, I had a hysterectomy."

"What does that have to do with sex?" Bill asked, like a big dummy.

"The loss of hormones is related to all kinds of problems: mood swings, insomnia, memory loss, irritability, fatigue, hot flashes, night sweats . . ."

I took a big breath.

"Depression, anxiety, bone loss, Alzheimer's, heart disease, and most relevant to this conversation, loss of libido and that dried up pinching sensation when . . ."

I scrunched up my face and Bill followed suit, his reaction an unspoken plea for another change of subject. I ignored it.

"Obviously, I'm OK now. I'm on B.H.R.T."

He looked confused. "B.H.R.T?"

"Bioidentical. Hormone. Replacement. Therapy," I stated slowly, nodding with each word to emphasize it.

Bill echoed the words back to me, nodding in mock mimicry.

"Bioidentical. Hormone. Replacement. Therapy. I've heard of it. I didn't know it could turn a woman into a sex fiend," he said with a snort.

"I am NOT a SEX FIEND!"

I heard some scraping sounds and turned to see the faces of nearby patrons who had adjusted their chairs to get a better sense of what was going on at the little table in the quiet corner.

"So sorry," I said to a young couple sitting behind us with their young children. Bill and I turned our backs to the audience and moved our chairs closer together.

"This isn't your mother's hormone replacement, Bill," I whispered. "These are all-natural hormone pellets injected under the skin: estradiol and testosterone."

"My mother never took any hormone replacement," Bill said smugly. "All she's ever needed is an aspirin. And why would a woman ever take testosterone?"

Not wanting to delve into a technical discussion on female biochemistry, I ignored him once again.

"A few days into it, I started feeling so much better: more confident at work, more productive at the gym, and my libido went through the roof. And sex wasn't uncomfortable anymore. I was as plump and juicy as a ripe peach."

Bill blushed and shifted in his seat, looking behind us, presumably to see if the young family were still in earshot. Fortunately, they had left.

"Is this too much information?" I asked coyly, trying not to smile and give my intentions away. For it had dawned on me. This subject matter, presented appropriately, would serve as an almighty aphrodisiac.

"Ah no, this is interesting, and it explains a lot," Bill said, taking a mouthful of ice water.

"Anyway, that's when I ran into a big problem. Lance. He had turned into a low-energy old man with no sex drive. We were essentially friends without benefits, and for the first time in all our married life, I really thought I might cheat on him, that we may end up divorced. But after six months of nagging, he agreed to see my doctor, and eventually he got pelleted with a heavy dose of testosterone."

Bill was giving me the shush sign but it was obvious my story had commandeered his attention. He handed the waitress his credit card without looking at the check.

"So, you would think happy ending, right?" I said. "I was sleeping like a baby, waking up full of energy, kicking ass at work, and Lance and I were going at it all the time. The sex got more and more adventurous and the orgasms more intense. It was better than it had ever been but then . . ."

I paused for dramatic effect.

"I noticed a sharp decline in Lance's interest, which physiologically didn't make sense, not with his T-level well over 1,000. But shortly thereafter, I caught him with . . . well . . . you've already heard that story, Bill."

I shrugged my shoulders and then tilted my head back and waited for the last drop of wine to make its way down to the lip of the glass and drop onto my tongue.

"Would you take him back?" Bill asked.

"You know, I would have, but he never asked."

"And since that time?" Bill asked tentatively, like he wasn't sure he wanted to hear the answer.

"Are you asking if I've been screwing around?"

"Well, I know it's none of my business," he said.

Before answering him, I made the calculation not to mention Marco.

"You were the first man I had sex with after the divorce. So no, I haven't been screwing around."

He said nothing, but I saw a wisp of relief on this face.

"What about you, Bill?" I asked. "I imagine you have no trouble getting a date and then some."

Obviously, I was inquiring as to how often he was feeding the kitty, but he got a faraway nostalgic look in his eyes.

"Dana and I made love every Sunday."

I smiled, rubbing my thumb on the top of his hand.

"Was Dana adventurous in bed?" I asked, trying to buoy the conversation.

"Not by your standards," he said, finally breaking into a smile.

"The reason I ask is, you seem to know your way around a woman's body pretty darn well."

"I read romance novels," Bill confessed in an embarrassed whisper.

"Well, hell. That explains it then!" I blurted, slapping the table, then I looped my arm through his and drew him closer.

"Have you ever taken testosterone?" I asked.

"No, but all of a sudden I'm thinking about it."

We giggled.

"You know, Bill, you blush a lot."

"And you don't!"

"I think I'm just very at ease with you . . . it's . . . well, it's nice."

And despite not being a fan of public displays of affection, I leaned towards him in an effort to kiss his cheek. He turned his head and our lips met. It was quick, soft, and electric.

CHAPTER SIXTEEN

Don't Say Fuck

"How about a ride?" Bill said.

I nodded an enthusiastic yes.

A horse-drawn carriage, a common site in old Montreal, was stationed just outside the restaurant door. It was on my to-do list, plus I needed time to digest that poutine. I waited while Bill got the particulars from the scruffy old driver, who was hunched over and dressed in black. The horse looked like his twin brother, heavy and worn, with a thick coat of black fur. The carriage, however, was shiny and new—white with red upholstery, large and open. It looked like it could seat up to four people, two and two, facing each other. Bill jumped in first, then gave me his hand and pulled me up. The sky was clear and alight with stars, but it was markedly colder than when we had left the hotel. He grabbed a blanket from a stack of three and put it across our laps. I heard a little giddy-up sound, and the old horse slowly pulled away from the curb.

In broken English, the driver asked if we would like to hear some history of the area. Bill said no thanks, and I guessed he wanted to continue our one-on-one uninterrupted.

For the next half hour, we took in the stunning architecture of old Montreal, the clip-clop of the horse's hooves adding to the romantic atmosphere. I wrapped my arms around Bill's waist between his soft cashmere polo and his sports jacket and put my head on his chest.

"This has been a wonderful evening," I said without looking up. "I'm so glad you came to visit."

"It's not over yet; it's not even 9 o'clock," he replied. "Anything special you would like to do?"

The old driver trained his ear in our direction.

"I want to do what I always want to do when I'm with you." I hugged him tight. "What do you want to do?"

Bill kissed the top of my head and dropped his voice to a deep hum.

"I want to make love to you."

Despite the load of adrenaline those words had just dumped into my body, I managed to look up at him and joke. "Sounds boring."

I smiled, and then put my head back down against his chest.

"I don't think so," he responded. "But it will definitely be different than the last time."

"I thought the last time was fan-fucking-tastic," I said, stifling a laugh.

Bill chuckled. "Well, I didn't say I didn't like it."

Once again, his voice modulated into a soft, serious, bass whisper.

"Every time I'm with you, Sally, it feels like the last time. I want to make love to you . . . before I don't have the chance."

I tilted my head up and he peered down at me and stroked my cheek.

"That kind of talk scares me, Bill."

"Scares me too."

And just then the horse came to a sudden stop; we were back in front of the restaurant. Bill helped me out of the carriage and took out his wallet to settle up with the driver. I offered to pay since he had picked up dinner, but he wouldn't let me.

"I'll pay you back somehow," I said.

"I know you will and very shortly." He winked and put his wallet back in his pocket. We put our arms around each other and walked the short distance back to the hotel.

"Do you need to get your things from the car?" I asked as we approached the front door.

"No, everything is in my room."

"You got a room?"

"Of course I got a room. My chances of spending the night with you are slim-to-none, aren't they?" he asked rhetorically. He stopped and smiled at me. "Yours or mine?"

I knew his room would make for an easier getaway but inexplicably replied, "Mine, in half an hour."

He looked surprised.

"OK then, I'll be there with bells on."

We parted, and I got in the elevator.

Be there with bells on was an old expression my grandmother used to use. I hadn't heard it in a long time. The elevator jerked up, bringing me back into the moment, but in that short diversion, there had been a shift in my feelings—a shift in Bill's direction.

Like the now infamous dress, the teddy provided allure, access, and cover. The stretch lace bodice strained under the weight of my humpty dumplings, my ample bottom bare beneath and barely masked by the sheer aqua blue rayon fabric. A white tag, visible along the right seam, read "Keep away from fire." Tonight, the mirror was exceptionally friendly, reflecting a radiant, relaxed me, a much different me than the previous Saturday when I was preparing for the pants-off dance-off with Marco. What a shitastrophe that had been.

Just then I heard a gentle knocking, like someone was lightly tapping the door with the knuckle of their index finger. The hairs on the back of my neck stood on end as I aroused with anticipation. I peered through the peep hole and Bill smiled and waved like he knew I was watching him. I opened the door to greet him. He was dressed comfortably in a long sleeve brown tee, untucked, and matching knit lounging pants and moccasins.

"Wow!" he said, giving me a big confidence boost. At my age, it's always an unexpected pleasure to get that hearty reaction. I took his hand, pulled him inside, and then wrapped my arms around his neck, tilting my head back, closing my eyes, waiting for him to kiss me. Eventually he did, his kiss soft and barely open. I pressed my tongue into his mouth, but he pulled away. When I reached for his waistband, he grabbed my wrist.

"What's wrong?" I asked.

He touched his forehead gently to mine.

"Let's slow it way down, Sally. We're doing it my way this time, remember?" he said quietly, caressing my arms and kissing my neck from my ear down along the top of my shoulder. Shudder.

Bill slow-walked his hands up the back of my legs, smiling slightly when discovering my nakedness under the dainty peignoir. There was no urgency though—well, not from him. When he finally led me to the bed and sat me down at the end of it, I tried to bury my face in his pants, but he got down on his knees before I could.

"Lie back," he commanded softly, coaxing my legs over his shoulders. I shut my eyes, waiting for his lips to make contact. And they did, along the inside of my thighs, alternating between them. After about two minutes of that torture, I began to squirm and shimmy, trying to angle myself onto his mouth.

"Relax, stay still," he said.

I was trying to but my body wouldn't cooperate, as relaxation is a foreign concept to me. Bill went back to the inside of my legs, this time very close to my slipperiness, and after an eternity, he stumbled upon it, pecking it gently, slowly, his mouth barely open, moving south to north along my aching chamber, and then south again. His lips finally rested on my entrance, and he kissed me wide, deep, and hungry.

"Oh yeah, Bill," I moaned. "That's perfect."

He set about pleasuring me with unparalleled skill, tugging on my magic button with his lips, exploring my happy valley with the tips of his fingers, almost overwhelming my senses. I was riding a glorious wave, a buoyed voyage just below full orgasm.

"Yes, yes, yes . . . keep it right there . . . right there," I mewed, but just as I was about to be swept up and over, Bill stopped his delightful diddling and started blowing cool air on me.

If this is a joke, it isn't funny.

"Bill, please, I'm so close," I said, maneuvering him into a headlock in an attempt to make contact with his mouth, his fingers, his cock-a-doodle-do, his anything.

"Stop that, Sally!" Bill protested, as he wrenched his head from between my quivering thighs. "Can you please just let me finish?"

"Isn't the goal to let ME finish?!" I responded, frustrated.

He leaned forward once more, pressing deep kisses into me, flicking his tongue on my swollen nub before stopping and blowing on me again, then that agonizing flicking. Finally, I couldn't stand it anymore. I raised myself up on my elbows.

"Bill, what the HELL are you doing down there?! This teasing is intolerable! There's no point complicating a good old fashioned fuck. Can we please get on with it?"

Bill stood up abruptly and parked his hands on his hips.

"Don't say fuck," he said sternly. "That's not what this is. Don't say anything. I just want you to feel."

Don't say fuck? While we're fucking? What the fuck?

Bill bent over me and kissed me lightly on the mouth, and I tasted myself on his lips. I grabbed on to his tremendous triceps and attempted to pull him down on top of me, but he jerked away, shaking his head.

Holy shit, I thought, I don't have the time or patience for this. I prefer Lance's Irish style of foreplay—Brace yourself Bridget! At least he got the job done. I crossed my arms over my chest, took another deep breath, and held it.

"Relaaaxxxx," Bill said again, breathing out the word mystically. But relax I could not, my body vibrating with tiny, tightly coiled up springs as if on a cocaine binge. The only way I was going to get through this was to distract myself with random thoughts.

Hockey: my favorite team, the Tampa Bay Lightning. The hottest hockey player, Henrik Lundqvist. Yeah, I bet HE could get the job done. Let's see, I need English muffins, marmalade, butter, soda water, and more wine. My right hip is bothering me again—I should check out that yoga studio up the street. Yoga, now that would help me relax. Studied breaths, in deeply through the nose, out slowly through the mouth, emptying the mind, visualizing the ragged mental and physical edges smoothing out of the body through the tips of the fingers and toes.

And in thinking about it and doing it, miraculously, it worked. Breathing out the random thoughts and tension made way for the warm voltaic energy spreading from Bill's mouth and hands. It surprised and delighted me.

"Bill." I exhaled his name, letting my legs fall limply to each side and stretching my arms above my head. "I can feel you, your energy traveling through me, filling me. It's wonderful."

As if he'd been waiting for those words, Bill stood and pulled his tee shirt over his head, unveiling that beautiful, bare, broad, bronzed chest. Then off came his pants, revealing his Montreal boxers with the fleur de lis on them. He got onto the bed and I rolled against him, reaching for his flaccid flesh flute. He brushed my hand away and whispered, "Not yet."

I closed my eyes and returned to the yogic breathing, concentrating only on that, letting Bill do all the work, kissing me on the neck, on the ears, on the cheek, and a wonderful long, open, wet one on the mouth, my mouth open and offering, but not answering in kind.

Skimming his hand across my neck and chest to my left breast, he pulled the stretchy lace down over it and moved his mouth onto my puckered nipple. Under normal circumstances, the caress of his tongue accompanied by the tender nibbling would have made me jump out of my skin, but in this state of total relaxation, I was able to more fully enjoy it.

Bill found the firm, round bolster against the headboard, placed it next to my hips, and gently rolled me up and over onto it, elevating my backside. My head, arms, and legs followed limply, like a rag doll's.

"Spread your legs for me, Sally."

Those words again. I didn't know if it was the words themselves or the way he said them, but it was almost enough to break me.

I did as directed, immersing myself in the moment rather than anticipating anything that might happen next. Bill slid the back of my fragile teddy up and began to massage me, pushing down on my lower back and up along my backbone. He was purposely delaying entry and strangely, that was OK with me.

I thought I might drift off under the command of his touch, but he took it to the next level, tickling me with his tongue along my spine, crawling his body closer to mine until he was bent over me, the bulk and weight and scent of him silently announcing his forthcoming invasion. When his hand slid between the bolster and my hips, and the soft pads of his fingertips found my mound, I had to fight to stay in the moment. When he guided his stiffness along my wet opening and then buried into me from behind, I felt a muted grunt reverberate from his throat against the back of my shoulder.

Bill's rhythmic in and out appeared carefully crafted to drive me to the edge of the pleasure precipice and hold me there. I clung to this position and swayed up against the I'm going to come cliff without losing my balance. It was so different, he was so different, and he was so right. This was not fucking.

And then he stopped and rolled me over off of the bolster. For a moment I was almost weightless, falling in slow motion onto what I imagined was a cloud, but it was just a pillow. I smiled up at him as he positioned me more appropriately, his knees wedging between mine, his skyward Skippy bouncing between my thighs. He rested against me and tenderly brushed the hair from my face.

"I want you to give yourself to me, Sally, body and soul this time. Will you do that for me?"

"I will," I whispered, not even sure what he meant, but completely under his spell.

Bill rose back up on his knees and looped his arms beneath my thighs, lifting them before entering me. Once again, he began his rhythmic rocking, slowly and deliberately, his loving energy spreading deeper into me, a pink aura beginning to form around him. He drew me into him through his penetrating eyes, and I could almost see his soul.

"Let me know," he said, his voice low, his manner controlled. I raised my legs higher, encouraging him to increase his rhythm and the depth of his stroke, and watched as he turned his attention, just a little, to satisfying himself, driving into me deeper, faster, intensity building, the shine of perspiration appearing on his upper body. Then his head fell forward and I heard him whisper my name. When he raised it, his eyes were completely dilated.

It was time.

I stretched my arms out to him, signaling my readiness, and he lowered himself onto me. I wrapped my arms around him, the back of my ankles under his ass pulling him forward as he continued to drive my Miss Daisy, his pelvis bearing down hard, pushing me to that edge. We were cheek-to-cheek, panting in unison like two runners pacing each other—uh . . . uh . . . uh . . . uh. Tingling, sweating, slipping and sliding, the delicate teddy twisting, tearing, and melting from the force of friction. Keep away from fire.

Then, in between labored breaths, he said it.

"Sally . . . I . . . I love you."

FLASH!

Deep inside . . . not electricity . . . but light . . . blinding white hot light. The support beneath me was giving way.

"Bill . . . I . . . I . . . I . . ."

"Say it," he moaned, softly.

"I . . . uh . . . uh . . . I . . ."

Gasping, spinning, balling the bedding in my hands in an effort to hold on.

"Say it!" he groaned, begging.

"Oh . . . God . . . Bill . . . I . . . I want you . . . so much . . ."

Falling, disoriented, tumbling over into a roiling orgasmic sea, the suck of a wave launching me back up, SLAM! back down, CRASH! on top of me. Fighting to cling to him, digging into his back, unable to hold the grip against the slick sweaty surface.

SCRAAATCCCHHH!

"JESUS!" he yelled, throwing his head back in pleasure or in pain, I couldn't tell, but it put a match to him. He moved with increasing need and passion as he grunted romance in my ear.

"Sally . . . feel me . . . feel my love. I want to give it to you . . . now . . . forever . . ."

And then he exploded.

"OH GOD BABY!!!"

And I did feel him, his heat, his light, his love, releasing into me, reigniting my orgasm, rocketing me back up and over again.

WHIP!

And then the white light, as if forced through a prism, shattered into a rainbow of flesh-rumbling frequencies, illuminating my insides like a Christmas tree.

"Bill . . . it's so good . . . it's so good," I whimpered, writhing beneath him, while his body, still grinding up into me, gave me all he had left.

My jellied arms dropped down and off Bill's glistening, sweaty back. He slowed his stroke, kissing me between breaths, making sure every bit of the experience was experienced before sliding gently to his side and resting his warm palm on my stomach.

I must have passed out because when I opened my eyes, I was under the covers, and he was up and dressed, sitting on the chair next to the bed, watching me.

"What time is it?" I asked, dreamily.

"Midnight."

"Really?" I glanced at the bedside clock to confirm.

Bill crawled back on the bed and I rolled on my side to face him, putting my hand on his cheek. I was afraid to speak.

"Bill . . . I . . . I've never . . ."

I felt a tear sneak out of the corner of my eye and drizzle down to the pillow. He brushed the wet trail with his thumb and kissed me tenderly on the mouth.

"Bill, you are an amazing lover." I managed to get the words out without breaking down, but I was trembling.

He smiled, pleased at my uncharacteristically emotional response. I turned my back to him so he could spoon me, and so he wouldn't see the next tear fall.

"Bill, can you write on my back?"

"With what?" he asked with a chuckle.

"With your finger."

"I can do that," Bill said, pecking at the back of my neck, setting off another ripple of goosebumps.

"Wait." I sat up and yanked the teddy over my head. I heard it rip but it didn't matter. It was already done for. I laid back down, naked now, not feeling the need to hide anything from him.

Bill covered me with the sheet and then gently eased it down my back to my waist. I felt his soft finger draw across my warm skin. I could tell what he was writing—exactly the same thing Lance had written so many times before him.

I love you Sally Shaw.

CHAPTER SEVENTEEN

Dear Sally

The hi-lo, wee-woo pulse wails of the city's emergency vehicles rattled the building, jarring me awake. I opened my eyes to look at the clock, but couldn't see it for the glare streaming in between the curtains. I picked up my cell. 10:30. Holy cow, I thought, I never sleep this late. Then I remembered, and I turned over to see if Bill was beside me. He wasn't. But next to where he should have been was the bedside table. The drawer was open, exposing the condoms: five unopened and one empty Magnum wrapper.

SHIT!

Had Bill seen the contents of the drawer? Of course he had—that's why he left the drawer open, and that's why he wasn't here!

Instinctively, I placed a Tim Horton's K-cup into the miniature coffee maker and started the brewing process. While the device snorted and shook, I checked my cell again. No texts, no emails. And then I saw it, a desiccated rose, presumably missed by the cleaning staff after my myrtling with Marco, lay on the coffee table. A note, folded neatly, was tented next to it.

Dear Sally,

Thank you for inviting me to Montreal. It was a magical evening for me, and I hope for you as well. My original intention in leaving this note was to let you know I had gone out to get us some French pastries and would return shortly. But after finding the paper and pen in the bedside table, I changed my mind.

I'm sure you know by now that I am hopelessly in love with you. I truly believe we are soulmates, and we're meant to be together, but unfortunately, you don't feel the same. I wish I could continue our relationship on your terms, but the thought of you in bed with another man is more than I can bear. You have been honest with me from the very beginning, so please don't feel guilty. I don't need or want an explanation. I'll be OK, but I won't be contacting you again.

All my love,

Bill

The Sunday morning church bells rang out, and this time, I answered the call. I pulled on some jeans and a hooded cardigan, laced up my sneakers, and ran out of the hotel towards the Notre Dame Basilica. I took a seat at the back of the church and knelt as the organist roared forth with medieval music that conjured both comfort and dread in me. Following along with the familiar ritual, I tried to keep my emotions in check by distracting myself with the stunning beauty of the church's interior: a kaleidoscope of blues, reds, purples, silver, and gold filled with hundreds of intricate wood carvings. But eventually, I depressed under the crushing weight of Bill's final communiqué. I watched as a long line of the faithful made their way to communion. I didn't join them.

The organist played "Oh Canada" for the recessional hymn, but I wasn't ready to stand, and I certainly couldn't break out in song. Rather, I remained kneeling with my head resting in the crook of my arm until the congregation had made their way out and the church fell silent. I stayed and prayed for guidance, and all of a sudden it came.

The whole friends-with-benefits thing is crap! I had been faithfully married for over 30 years. Why would I think I could change so drastically? I felt the electricity between us right from the get-go and let Bill know it by my actions, but when he responded, I turned him away just to prove to myself that I could.

And then last night when I gave him every indication I had changed my ways and believed he was the one, he was slapped in the face with my transgression with Marco. I'd be lucky if he ever spoke to me again, but I had to try. I had to confess the one misguided and uninspiring zipless and tell Bill how I really felt—that I loved him and wanted only him.

I walked out into the cold, blinding October sun and breathed the icy wind into my lungs, welcoming the sting of it. I marched the return route to my hotel, feeling alive and with new clarity of purpose. I didn't know exactly where Bill was, but I knew it wasn't far to Burlington, and so he was probably already at the airport trying to get an earlier flight out. It was possible he was already in the air. Too nervous to call him, but committed nonetheless, I took the easy way out and sent him a text.

Me: Will you let me explain?

A half hour later, I changed my clothes and headed for the gym, confident a message would be waiting for me when I returned.

It was an atypical workout: walking trance-like on the treadmill, re-living the romance, the special moments, the intense love-making. But that trip down memory lane was short-lived, driven from my consciousness by Marco and his strapping sidekick,

Long Dong Silver. Tears ensued, along with an all-out sprint. Winded, I composed and slowed to a walk, but guilt fueled another breathless run. One hour later, physically and emotionally bankrupt, I headed back to my room.

I took a deep breath and picked up my phone—a text. Elation! Then letdown. Then anger rising from frustration.

Lance: Can you talk?

Me: About what?

Lance: Life insurance

Me: What about it?

Then it rang, but my sweaty finger couldn't make the necessary contact to answer it. I was just about to throw the frickin' thing against the wall when it finally connected.

"What the hell is it, Lance?!"

"Sally, what's wrong?"

"Nothing! What do you want?"

"Are your parents OK?"

"YESSSSSSS!!!!"

"Is this work related?"

"NO! You have ten seconds to tell me why you're calling."

"Well . . . I . . . thought it was about time I changed my life insurance beneficiary . . . to Margarita."

"MARGARITA?!!! THAT'S her name?"

"Yes, I've told you that more than once, Sally. It's Spanish for Margaret."

"Are you sure it isn't Spanish for tequila, triple sec, and LIME JUICE?!"

"Look, I just wanted to do you the courtesy of telling you I'm changing my primary beneficiary election to her."

"Our daughters should be your primary beneficiaries, Lance. You promised me!"

"They are, Sally, they are, on everything else, even the new house. You have to understand how vulnerable Margarita feels. If I walked out on her tomorrow, she'd have nothing to show for time served."

"Has anyone told you lately that you are a colossal asshole Lance?"

"I just . . . I have to put her name on something."

"Why don't you put it on the bathroom wall at your country club, or is that how you two met?!"

CLICK.

How was it Lance knew just when to worm his way back into my story and burrow under my skin?

When our matrimonial bond was dissolved by his disaffection, I grieved, but unlike a death, a divorce doesn't grant the griever the opportunity to accept and move on—not when a long and fruitful history demands the lines of communication stay open. I still had to take his calls, and worse, he had just purchased a McMansion only two miles down the road from my little beach house, boosting the odds of an encounter at the grocery store or a nearby restaurant. Just like eternal damnation, the torture would never end. And having learned that hard lesson, here I was, staring at the phone waiting for Bill's call, and primed to parachute into the clutches of monogamy once again.

Love is truly a cruel master.

I fought all week to stay focused on work but was distracted by my inability to get in touch with Bill. He wasn't answering my texts or emails, and his email autoreply was responding "Out on personal business." Had he left Montreal and gone on vacation? He never mentioned that. By the end of the week, still hearing nothing from him, I began to panic and I called Laura.

As soon as she said hello, I broke down in hysterics, completely unhinged. I spat out Two-Story or Ranch? and described that evening's unfortunate end, and then I hit her with Dear Sally. By the end of story time, Laura was almost as unglued as I was.

"Sally, I've never seen . . . I mean . . . heard you this broken up in my life. You weren't this upset when Lance left. You need to get a hold of yourself! You and your stupid Smokin' Hot Sex is Enough manifesto!"

"Well . . . sniffle . . . sniffle . . . it works for you!" I boo-hooed like a teenager.

"Well OBVIOUSLY, I'm not in love!"

"I'll be OK, Laura," I said deflated and finally cried out. "I'm just so homesick. I'll be back in two more days. Can we do happy hour on Monday instead of waiting until the end of the week?" I asked, not revealing the plan I was already hatching.

"You got it, girl."

Laura pulled into my driveway and I climbed in her car with a six-pack of Goose Island IPA, one of her favorites. I was trying to soften her up. She wasn't so thrilled when I told her happy hour would be spent drinking beer in her car as we staked out Bill's condo.

"What is the purpose of a stakeout?" she asked. "Just knock on his damn door!"

"I can't do that. I need to know what's going on with him before I make my next move."

"You're always so effin dramatic," Laura said under her breath as she pulled out onto the beach highway. When we realized we didn't have an opener, she turned into a fast food parking lot, jumped out, and popped the cap off a beer bottle against a stop sign bracket. I handed her another bottle, and she repeated this time-tested method. About five minutes later, we rolled into the parking lot of the Soft Sands condo complex.

"Over there," I said, pointing to a spot across from the front entrance, "and back it in." It was 4:45. I was prepared to wait until 6. By then it would be almost dark, and we'd be out of beer.

At 5:04, a light rain began to fall, dappling the windshield, obscuring our view. When Laura turned the key in the ignition so she could close the windows and activate the wipers, her headlights flashed and lit up the condo entrance just as Bill stepped out the door. He looked directly at us.

"Shit!" I said, flattening against the seat, going horizontal. "That's him!"

Laura described the scene through a clenched jaw, like a ventriloquist.

"He just opened a big umbrella. He's holding the door for someone. It's a woman."

"Does she have long black hair?" I asked, my heart starting to race a rhythm in the back of my throat.

"I can't tell, the umbrella is in the way . . . Looks like he's walking her to her car . . . He has his hand on her back . . . He's opening her car door . . . They're hugging . . . and now I think they might be . . . I'm not sure . . . but it's more than just a friendly hug."

"I'm too late . . . it's too late," I said with a whimper, my eyes starting to well up.

Laura gave my forearm a compassionate squeeze.

"OK, Sally, she's driving away . . . oh SHIT! He's coming over here. Sit up!"

"Oh my God, Laura," I said, adjusting the seat and wiping my eyes on my shirt sleeve.

Bill was approaching, bending a little to get a better view. Laura rolled down my window and he put his hand on the wet ledge.

"Sally?" he said, waving a little wave. Laura waved back and nervously drained her beer.

"Ah . . . hi Bill . . . um . . . this is my best friend, Laura."

"Hi," he said, plainly baffled. Then to me, "What are you doing here?"

Unprepared for this confrontation, I had to free-style it.

"We were just road tripping and I had told Laura about your condo renovation, so we pulled in on the off chance we'd catch you and could take a look. I've tried contacting you a few times, but you didn't respond to my texts, and your email autoreply says you're out on personal business."

It made absolutely no sense considering what had happened in Montreal.

"Oh," said Bill, accepting the nonsense. "I lost my phone somewhere between Montreal and the Burlington airport, so I had it disabled. Then I decided to change carriers. I don't have the same number now. And yeah, I've been taking time off to manage the renovation."

Laura reached around the back of her seat and pulled another beer out of the little cooler, then realized she couldn't open it.

"You know, you girls shouldn't be driving around drinking," Bill said, looking concerned.

"Old habits die hard, Bill," I said, trying to sound cool when I was actually in A-fib.

Then, awkward silence. Laura began to adjust the mirrors.

"Well, since you're here, would you like to come up and see it?" he offered, still confused.

Laura turned towards him. "I really can't—I have to feed the cat," she said abruptly. "You go ahead, Sally."

"Well, how would I get back home?"

"Take Uber," Laura said, digging a finger into my thigh, encouraging me to get out of the car and go with him.

"I'll drive you home, Sally," Bill said flatly.

And at that moment I realized, although the outcome I was hoping for was highly unlikely, at least I could try and set things straight.

"Well, I'd really like to see what you've done . . . you know . . . if it's no problem."

"Hand me those empties," Bill said, reaching into the car and taking them from Laura. "I'll get rid of them."

"Thanks, Bill," Laura said, smiling. "Very nice meeting you. Hey Sally," she added, wide-eyed as I opened the door to get out of the car, "call me."

Laura pulled out of the parking lot and Bill and I walked to the condo entrance, stopping by the recycle bin so he could drop the two empty bottles into it. He entered a code at the condo entrance and I heard a click, then he opened the door for me.

"I'm up one level," he said, shaking the umbrella and pointing to a circular staircase with the tip of it. We walked up in uneasy silence.

He opened his unlocked door and I stepped into a very open space that drew my gaze through a wall of glass to the open ocean—a multimillion dollar view. Despite the drop cloth, paint cans, and stray tiles lying around, I was awestruck, and instinctively I slipped off my flip-flops to avoid contaminating the area.

"A couple of weeks ago, this layout was all cut up," Bill said, walking into the living area, pointing here and there. "My decorator, Robin, had the wall between the kitchen and dining room taken out, as well as the wall between the living area and a third bedroom, which I gave up to get the expanded view. The kitchen was a complete gut; it's much more functional now. The two bathrooms should be finished in the next couple of weeks. What do you think?" he asked proudly, trying not to puff up too much.

"I love it, Bill. This Robin—is that her name? She did a great job."

"Yeah. Robin Robards."

"Is she the woman Laura and I saw you with just now in the parking lot?"

"Yes," Bill said, swallowing the word.

"Hmmm." I nodded. "I'm guessing you two have something going on. I know that's none of my business."

Bill furrowed his eyebrows, apparently struggling to define their relationship.

"We've dated a couple of times . . . Sally, what are you really doing here?"

Now it was my turn to struggle.

"I . . . I . . . want . . ." I closed my eyes, searching for the right words.

"You want to have sex with me," Bill said quietly.

"No . . . yes . . . of course . . . but I mean it's . . . it's more than that . . . I want to talk to you . . . about Montreal."

Bill folded his arms across his chest and studied me for a moment, then a strange look came over him and he walked over to me, cupped my face, and kissed me. His electric mouth, opening and closing in a rolling motion over mine, started a wave undulating through my body. I couldn't help melting and moaning into him, but as soon as I did, he broke the kiss, took me by the hand, and led me down the hall and into his bedroom. It was dark and I couldn't read his expression, but his grip on me was stone cold and determined. Before I could get my bearings, he yanked his tee shirt off and threw it on the chair.

Then he pulled his shorts down and kicked them into a corner. His abrupt and exaggerated body language suggested hostility, an emotion I'd never seen in him.

Bill took two aggressive steps towards me and I held out my arms to embrace him, but he grabbed the hem of my tee shirt and clumsily worked it over my head. I could see his face now—he looked like a stranger. He hugged me to him and whispered passionless in my ear.

"I know what you want, Sally."

I swallowed hard, unable to speak. Part of me wanted to stop this, talk it out, and set the record straight. But part of me wanted him to consume me, and that part was winning.

Bill sat on the side of the bed and pulled me down on his lap, maneuvering my knees on either side of him. His movements were procedural and robotic. I put my arms around his neck and held onto him as he unhooked my bra.

"Bill," I said, bending back to look him in the eyes, "about Montreal. Please let me explain."

"I don't want to talk about Montreal," he said, a hitch in his voice, and then he lifted me up, spun around, and lost his balance, dropping me down on the bed on my back and tumbling forward onto me.

"For God's sake, Bill! What's gotten into you?!" I said, pushing him off of me.

He stumbled to his feet, opened the bedside table drawer, pulled out a condom, and tore through the wrapper with his canines. His typically inviting aqua eyes had taken on a dark and brooding nature, but behind the barricade of bitterness, I detected pain.

He's not a very good actor.

Then I noticed something in his hand. It was an orange-colored cock ring. He stretched the ring wide with his two hands, positioned it over his droopy dingus, and fiddled with it for a bit, visibly irked that it wasn't doing what he wanted it to do. Then I heard it buzz to life. Under the circumstances, the addition of an adult novelty product struck me as absurd, but nothing about the moment was funny so I didn't laugh.

"This is what you came here for, isn't it, Sally," Bill said, expressionless as he climbed on top of me, the vibrating ring skipping an uneven beat between us.

"I came here to talk to you, Bill," I said, putting his face in my hands and trying to shake some life into it. "Why aren't you listening to me?!"

He didn't respond but rather reached around and under me, and holding me tight, rolled over on his back, rotating me on top. My dueling banjos dangled above him. He grabbed them and squeezed, his touch strangely unfamiliar. I swatted at his awkward grip, and for a few seconds we appeared to be playing a half-witted game of patty cake.

"Bill! Can we stop for a minute?!"

"Fine!" he snapped. "Sorry I couldn't do it for ya!" Then he underlined his resignation with a swift slap on my ass, and like a scratch on a DVD, it freeze-framed the action, leaving us locked in an uncomfortable stare—the silence interrupted by the sporadic drone of the vibrator.

In a flash I was off the bed gathering my things as Bill began his battle with the ring. I bolted down the hall, shoving the bra in my purse, then pulling my tee shirt on and sliding into my sandals. I almost made it out the front door, but Bill gave chase and slammed it shut.

He stood there in his boxers, forlorn and almost weepy, but before anything could be said, there was a knock. I saw alarm in his eyes, and as if he knew what was about to happen, he spun and rushed back down the hall towards his bedroom. A key turned in the lock, and the front door opened.

CHAPTER EIGHTEEN

I've Never Done Anal

"William? It's me," she said as she stepped inside, and I was face-to-face with the mysterious trespasser in the *SEA Family Newsletter*.

She was tall, pale, slim, with very narrow and pointed features that were punctuated by her long black hair, now pulled back tight into a French twist. She was professionally dressed in a modern gray pantsuit, and with the help of a bra designed to make as much out of a small set as possible, her breasts were pressed together and up, and they peeked seductively out of her yellow silk shirt.

I was immediately threatened: not by her beauty, not by her style, but by her years. She was young, very young, Margarita young.

How could he.

"Oh!" she said, startled. "Who are you?"

Overwhelmed by Bill's heartless reception and now this unwelcome encounter with the shiny new object of his affection, I couldn't speak. I had to get out. I stepped past her and reached for the door handle with my unsteady hand.

"Sally, WAIT!" I heard Bill shout, and I turned towards his anxious voice. He was properly dressed now, articulating an explanation as he walked briskly towards us.

"Robin, this is Sally. She works at SouthEast Atlantic too. I wanted to show her how the remodel was going," he said pretty convincingly, albeit somewhat breathlessly.

She didn't shake my hand and instead focused all of her energy on Bill.

"I was just here; you didn't say anything about a guest," she said, her dark eyes flashing. "I forgot my paint color wheel," she continued, walking into the kitchen and lifting it off of the counter. Then she made her way to Bill's side. Her spectator pumps gave her a height advantage over him. She snaked her arm through his and the corners of her mouth lifted slowly into the same victorious expression I'd seen on Margarita.

And that's when my stress response revised from flight to fight.

"I dropped in without notice," I said, just this side of friendly. "You've done a wonderful job." Then I crossed my arms, locked eyes with her, and added, "I could live here."

Robin straightened and stepped in front of Bill like a mother cat protecting her kitten. I thought I heard her growl. Then she turned towards him and put her arms on his shoulders. I couldn't see his face but I could feel the fear emanating from him, like he was afraid he might have to break up a cat fight and there was no hose nearby.

"Now, don't forget about tomorrow, William," she said, wrapping her arms tightly around his neck. "Dinner with the Dingles down at the marina. I can't wait to show you my makeover of their cabin cruiser."

She pressed her red stained lips against Bill's cheek like she was trying to leave a mark, and she did. Bill, frozen in place, made no move to touch her. He looked to be in extreme discomfort, and as far as I was concerned, it looked good on him.

"Can I show you out, Sally?" Robin asked coolly.

"I can find my way out. Thanks, though," I said.

She opened the door and shot one more look at

me, conveying the message "He's mine." Then the door closed behind her, and Bill and I stared at each other as we listened to the click, click, click of her high heels diminish.

"She's so young," I said, shaken by the drama of it all.

"She's Lisa's niece," Bill said softly. "Lisa suggested she do the remodel . . and . . . well . . . one thing led to another."

He stared down at the floor then picked up a small piece of stray tile and tossed it in the sink.

"Why does she call you William? Does she think that makes her sound more mature?" I asked, having accepted the bouncy-bouncy but still grappling with the conspicuous age disparity.

"It's not serious, Sally; not for me," Bill said, measured. "She's had a crush on me for years. I don't know why."

"I do," I said quietly.

"Well . . . after Montreal . . . I figured why not," he said.

"Why not indeed," I said, nodding in understanding.

"Listen, I want to apologize for what happened just before she showed up," he said, becoming animated. "As soon as you came through that door, I got it in my head to . . . well . . . you know . . . just a wham bam thank you ma'am, then rush you out of here, hoping you would feel used like I've felt. It was juvenile and mean."

Wham bam thank you ma'am?

"And spanking you like that—that was awful. I'm so sorry."

"So, I'm guessing Robin likes it rough," I said, softening a little.

"No," Bill said, blushing crimson. "She's the hitter, and I've got the bruises to prove it."

I grinned in spite of myself and pointed at his cheek.

"She . . . ah . . . left her mark."

Bill rubbed the heel of his hand across his cheek, smearing the red around.

"Did I get it?"

"No," I said, taking a more deliberate tone. "Bill, I'm going to ask you this one last time. Can we please sit down for just a minute so I can talk to you about Montreal?"

"Of course, yes," Bill said, looking relieved that I hadn't slapped his face and walked out already. Almost skipping into the living room and gesturing to a chair, he added, "I'll have a glass of wine if you'll join me. Sauvignon Blanc?"

"OK." I smiled, weakly. "If you insist."

I collected my thoughts as Bill washed the lipstick from his face and poured the wine. When he returned, he took a seat on the edge of the couch. I shifted to face him.

"I know you left Montreal because you saw the open condom wrapper in the drawer, and you surmised, correctly, that I'd slept with someone else."

Bill looked down at the floor like he really didn't want to relive the Magnum moment. I got off the chair and sat beside him on the couch, squeezing his hand.

"Bill, I'm going to tell you a story that you will not believe, and I'm going to tell you the end of the story first, and that is I'm through with this ridiculous notion that I can live happily-ever-after having meaningless sex. I can't . . . I know that now."

Bill looked back up at me, and I saw a glimmer of hope in his eyes.

"This all goes back to my marriage failure, and I'm ready to admit there were things I did to contribute to it. I've been afraid of failing again, and that's kept me from committing to another relationship. I'm not saying I want to get married, but I'm sure I could be monogamous with the right man . . . with you . . . if you're still interested in trying."

"That's all I needed to hear," Bill said adoringly. He attempted to put his arms around me, but I gently pushed him away and stood up.

"No. You have to listen to my story. It's a doozy."

Bill picked up his wine glass and like a good sport settled back to watch and listen. And for the next 15 minutes, animated more than I had ever been, I recounted Swinging Boom and watched Bill gasp, and then laugh, and then shake his head in incredulity.

Obviously, I left some particulars out; things that would have stung him.

"I don't know why you're working at SEA," Bill said. "You should be a writer; you have a great imagination."

"No imagination necessary. That all actually happened."

"Well then I was right. You're a cougar," Bill said, stifling a grin.

"I am NOT a COUGAR, Bill! And if I were you, I wouldn't bring up age," I said, wagging my finger at him. "Robin could pass for the captain of a high school volleyball team!"

Bill chuckled. "All right, a truce. No more talking about past indiscretions."

He picked up his cell phone, touched the screen a couple times, then brought it to his ear. He raised his finger to his lips in a preemptive shush.

"Hi Robin. Yeah, hey, I'm not going to be able to make that dinner tomorrow with your friends . . . no . . . no, I'm OK, just . . . it's not going to work out . . . no, I mean us . . . we're not going to work out. I'm really sorry. I should be telling you this in person. No . . . no . . . now you know that's not true . . . we have nothing in common . . . not even that."

I imagined them doing THAT and Bill glanced nervously in my direction like he read my mind.

"Please forgive me, Robin, and listen, there's no reason we can't still do business together because the bathrooms aren't finished and—"

I heard a "FUCK YOU!" as he moved the cell away from his head to avoid getting an earful. He looked at it. She had hung up.

Bill set the phone down and picked up his wine.

"Here's to a new beginning," he said, clinking his glass against mine.

"I think we should celebrate," I said, throwing my leg over his lap, straddling him. "Wanna go back in the bedroom?"

"Geez, you're so aggressive," he said jokingly, running his hands up under my skirt, "and no underwear."

"I don't wear underwear on the weekends."

"It's Monday," he quipped.

"Yeah, but it's a long weekend. I had the day off."

I grinned, stood up, and offered him my hand, and he rose to join me. We swallowed the last of our drinks, put the glasses down, and got to it, and as we made our way down the long hall, the benign flirtatious banter morphed into carnal greed.

Bill coaxed me against the wall and kissed my neck, tickling me, and I giggled and bent my head against his to try and stop it.

"Hey," I said, "I want you to use that dick ring thing Robin brought over here."

Bill chuckled, pulling me away from the wall and twirling me around a couple of times as we danced towards his bedroom. "How do you know Robin brought it over? Maybe it's mine."

"Doubtful, since you can barely figure out how to turn it on and off," I said as he jockeyed behind me and pinned me against the opposite wall, flexing his hips up under my plentiful posterior. "And by the way, can we speed up the sex a little?" I asked, smiling to myself, tilting my head back against his shoulder, as he smoothed his hands around the front of my thighs and up under my skirt. "That rogering in Montreal took forever. I almost fell asleep."

"As I recall, that rogering brought you to tears," he murmured in that low base whisper as his fingers crept closer to the aching apex of my legs.

"Yeah well, whatever. We're going to have to go faster," I said, feigning disinterest but feeling the urgency building as his semi grew stiff against my backside.

"I don't think faster is going to be a problem," Bill said, spinning me around to face him.

He pulled his shirt over his head and I put my hands on his copper chest and felt warmth radiate up my arms. He placed his hands on the wall on either side of my shoulders and pressed his hardness against me, then rubbed his nose back and forth across mine, Eskimo style. I could feel the intensity of his affection for me. It wasn't scary; it was comforting, like a big bowl of homemade macaroni and cheese.

Bill waltzed me through the bedroom door and we collapsed onto the bed, reaching for each other in the dim light. He laid back and pulled his shorts down, and his blood-filled boner snapped up and slapped his stomach. He found the cock ring and stretched it over himself, then struggled again to turn it on. It finally stuttered to an uncertain start.

"Your chariot awaits, milady," he said as he gently rolled me on top of him. I lifted my skirt and closed my eyes and sat back slowly as he maneuvered his muscle of love inside my silky center. It felt so good, I was afraid to move.

I pulled the tee off over my head and Bill reached up to corral my carumbas. This time, his touch was warm, tender, and familiar. I moved against him carefully at first, brushing against the vibrating ring, getting used to it, then faster, grinding against it, quickly closing in on the wham. Bill smiled up at me. He was enjoying me, enjoying him.

"Come here," he said, interrupting my launch to Mars as he pulled me down to kiss me and then rolled on top of me. It was dizzying. He pulled out, pushing back up onto his knees.

"I just want to increase the speed on this thing," he said, as he once again fiddled with the cock ring. He finally found the turbo setting, and his eyes went wide as the ring hummed and hopped on his peter like a worn out washing machine on spin cycle.

Bill wrapped his arms under my shoulders and closed in on me, working his knees between my legs, the muffled buzzing of the cock ring vibrating against my inner thighs. We stilled and smiled at each other, understanding this would be our first time—our first time knowing for sure there would be a next time.

"You're mine, Sally" he murmured low in my ear, his tone deliberate and decidedly possessive. At first that sentiment unsettled me, but I made the conscious decision to embrace the change he was foisting on me because I couldn't bear the alternative.

Twitching with anticipation while I waited for Bill's divining rod to discover my wellspring, hot honey drizzled from me, sizzling like pancake batter on a red hot griddle. He pushed into my hungry cave until the cock ring's quavering capsule crawled up under my hood and tasered my clitoris.

"Oh my GOD!" tore from my chest, and reflexively I arched, flinging my arms overhead, banging my knuckles against the headboard. I grabbed on to the rails and raised my legs and hips, and Bill sank farther into me, riding the ring around and down hard against me.

I'm going to buy a dozen in every color, along with a case of batteries.

"Oh yeah . . . that's it . . . just like that," I groaned as Bill began a nice gentle humping motion, both of us getting used to the added stimulation, as well as the somewhat distracting buzzing sound.

"Sally, I've wanted this . . . wanted you . . . again . . . so much."

There was something about the way he communicated when he made love to me. It made me feel like the sexiest, most exciting, most desirable woman in the world, and it made me want him more than anything.

"I'm ready for you Bill," I whispered.

Bill moved his hands under my fleshy bottom and pulled me closer. He picked up speed, increasing the action until he was practically lifting me off the bed with each thrust, humping the pulsating ring into my iron nub until my whole body was vibrating with the same frequency. As I inched to just this side of the point of no return, he whispered breathlessly in my ear.

"I love you, Sally."

"Bill . . . I . . . I . . ."

"Say it," he groaned, moving wildly faster, trying to drive the words he wanted to hear, out of me.

"I . . . I . . . oh GOD!"

"SAY IT!" Bill said, loud, passionate, close to losing himself in me.

"I love you, Bill . . . so much . . . and I . . . I . . . I'm . . ."

Bill reached up with both hands and grabbed the headboard rails, flattening himself on me, changing his angle into me, and slowing it down, giving us both the opportunity to really live each other's experience. I grunted in rhythm with each of his deep, deliberate thrusts and readied for his release, waiting for it to trigger my own. He gasped, then stiffened, then let me have it.

"Oh my GOD! YEAH! BABY!" he roared, burying his face in the pillow to muffle the sound of the glorious torture, as he flexed his fiery fountainhead into me, the accompanying supercharged flash of white hot lightning driving a guttural scream from my core as I convulsed into climax under the weight of his own.

And then it was quiet, except for an intermittent buzzing as the battery slowly died and the cock ring sputtered to a stop. Bill wrestled it off.

We lay still for a while, basking in the wake of our love-making, giving me the opportunity to absorb the magnitude of this earthquake that had just catapulted me from single status to *In a Relationship*. The fact was, Bill's passion, fueled by his intense love for me, was overwhelming, and I struggled to beat back a flood of emotion. While I knew he would become a constant craving, I also knew I would have to get used to this feeling of uncomfortable vulnerability, a feeling I had been so steadfast in avoiding. This would be the cost of keeping him in my bed. Right at this moment, I was willing to pay it.

I reached for him in the dark, slapping the mattress a few times until I finally landed on his hand— it was limp. I rolled over against him; he looked like he was passed out.

"Billllllll," I cooed in his ear, "Wake up."

He turned his head towards me and opened his beautiful blue eyes, glazed over with that just-been-laid haze.

"I'm hooked," I mewed, nuzzling his neck. "I can't wait for round two."

"Ah . . . round two?" he asked, uncomfortably surprised. "How about dinner and a movie first?"

"You wanted me and you got me, Bill. Now we need to make up for lost time."

"I've got the entire series of *Dallas* on DVD. That would be fun to get into, don't you think?" he said, grinning. Then he rolled to meet me.

"I think I'm going to have to call that doctor of yours and get some testosterone," he said with a wink.

"Good idea. And while you're at it, get some Viagra. That stuff really puts lead in the pencil. Now, how are you going to beat that last performance?"

"Well," Bill said, pretending to seriously consider the question, "I don't know if I've ever told you this, but I've never done anal."

About the Author

Bridget Doone makes her debut as a comedic erotic fiction writer with *Sally Rides Single*, the first in the Sally Rides Series. Originally from Ontario, Canada and now working as a network engineer in Florida, Bridget weaves Canadian landscapes and experiences into her Florida beaches-based romantic entanglements. She lives vicariously through her heroine, Sally, an engineer facing retirement and navigating life, love, and sex after 50 with a heavy dose of humor.

Bridget lives with her husband of many years. They have two grown daughters.

To learn more about Bridget and read excerpts from her next installment in the series, *Sally Rides Double*, visit her website at www.bridgetdoone.com.